THE RAINMAKERS

THE RAINMAKERS

by E. J. Bird

Carolrhoda Books, Inc./Minneapolis

LIBRARY OF CONGRESS CATALOGING-IN-PUBLICATION DATA

Bird, E.J.
  The rainmakers / by E.J. Bird.
     p.   cm.
  Summary: An Anasazi boy living long ago in the cliffs of the American Southwest shares a series of adventures with his pet bear and his best friend during his eleventh summer.
  ISBN 0-87614-748-1
  [1. Pueblo Indians—Fiction. 2. Indians of North America—Southwest, New—Fiction. 3. Bears—Fiction.]
I. Title.
PZ7.B51192Rai   1993
[Fic]—dc20   92-29789
                                                        CIP
                                                         AC

Manufactured in the United States of America

1   2   3   4   5   6   98   97   96   95   94   93

This book is in memory of Dr. Dean Brimhall and Dr. Walter Cottam. They were my special Ph.D. friends, my campfire and good-talk friends. They taught me much about this beautiful part of the country.

Foreword

omewhere in our great Southwest, there is a deep canyon cut into the red sandstone by millions of years of frost and floods, and the storms of long, cold winters. It is wild and lonesome there, and the high walls press in upon you, leaving only a slit of sky above. On clear days, when seen from below, the sky is a dark, wonderful blue, almost purple. In a narrow place high above your head, there is a crack in the rock where a spring of good water spills and winds its way over the slickrock and gravel until it disappears in the sand a half-mile down the canyon. It is here the ferns and wild columbine grow, and the swallows come for mud to build their nests. Cattle and wild things drink here and foul the place, and you can see their tracks where they've muzzled the water. Everything is very still—as if something mysterious is hidden somewhere near. Sounds bounce off the walls and come back to you in strangely muted echoes. Ghosts are about. You can almost feel them watching. Sometimes you can hear strange sounds carried on the wind that prowls the canyons—sounds that remind you of old forgotten songs, or sounds like music played on the low keys of a flute. There are watching eyes in every small wind cave carved in the slick red walls, and behind the huge rocks and rubble that have fallen from above and now lie scattered on the canyon floor. You know they are old ghosts that have lost their power, but you move carefully so you won't disturb them.

Down the canyon, not far from the spring and above you twenty feet or so, there is a deep arch cut in the cliff's hard face. This arch almost hides an old, abandoned village made of worked over rocks, a few wood timbers, and broken clay mortar. Rooms are piled on top of rooms, some big, some small, with gaping holes that once were door and window openings. Eight hundred years ago, this was the home of maybe ten families of a tribe called the Moquis by present-day ranchers and Indians. Our history books call them the Anasazi.

The Anasazi were a small, tough breed that farmed the high, flat country and hid their homes in the canyons for protection from the weather, and probably from the raiding plains tribes far to the east and north. All the Anasazi people, from all the

villages in this beautiful canyon country, left suddenly somewhere around our calendar year 1250 A.D. No one knows why or exactly where they went. They left behind the broken walls of their villages, some shattered pots and scraps of woven baskets, and a few painted and scratchy pictures on the smooth surfaces of the canyon walls.

This village by the spring was once a live and safe place where small, brown-skinned people ate and slept, and made beautiful jugs of clay, and wove baskets from the long, hard fibers of the desert. It was a place of barking dogs, crying children, and women calling. It was a place alive with the coming and going of an active tribe who ate corn and squash, and kept turkeys in pens near their rock houses. It was a place of old men, chanting in high, thin voices to the rhythm of drums beating—beating back the shadows of the night.

The things that live here now are bats, and cougars, and staring lizards with mobile eyes that watch for insects in the afternoon sun of summer. You can see through the broken doorway into the dark room. That's it—the one to the left where a morning dove had once built a nest of broken twigs. A few of the walls have fallen, and the stones lie scattered on the ground. And the sounds—the only sounds you hear are the splash of water from the spring, and the sighing wind as it searches through the empty rooms of the long-forgotten village—but if you'll only listen, you'll hear the whispering of the ghosts.

As an artist, I've always stood in awe when looking at the beautiful paintings and drawings the old ones placed on the stone walls of our canyons. I have never tried to inject any "meaning" of my own into their artwork—I leave that to the experts. I try to look and enjoy what they left for us. They used clays mixed with animal fat for the paintings, and the clay hardened and became almost part of the rock itself. The drawings were scratched or chipped into the top, weathered part of the rock, exposing a lighter layer beneath. And they are very, very old, some dating back a thousand years or more. They have lasted all this time, some getting lighter year by year through exposure to the sun. Some are entirely gone now, or destroyed in part by a kind of people who somehow cannot bear to see a perfect thing remain so.

Once, at a beautiful painted panel, I looked down, and there on a flat ledge was the outline of a small foot. The artist had scratched an outline, and then, with a hard, sharp rock, had chiseled into the ledge a pattern of his foot. And I put my own foot over the tracing and knew that I stood exactly where the artist who had made it stood. This brought me to wonder about the people who were there so long before me. I wondered what they were like, how they lived, and what they were thinking in those far-off times.

After many years of thinking and reading and wondering how it really was, I decided to put my thoughts together in writing. So I pass them on to you in this small book.

No one knows for certain how it actually was with the Anasazi. Some things were passed on to their descendants, the Hopi and other Pueblo peoples, but one can only guess as to the Anasazi's rituals and customs and about their daily lives. This is what I

have done in my writing—this is how I think it was in that long-ago time.

For those of you who give me less than passing grades in Anthropology 101 and the life and times of the ancient peoples of our great Southwest, I give to you a small black bear who, when he raises his arms and dances like a bird, can make it rain.

Chapter
ONE

The first harsh notes from the new flute sent the jay-bird that had been watching from a dead limb off through the tall trees, screeching and fussing as it went.

"It's a great wonder to me," said the grandfather, "how a beautiful thing like a flute can make such horrible sounds. Here, may I see it?" The old man took it and held it in his hands. "It's made from the leg bone of a deer or big-horned sheep," he said. "Did you see the carvings? Here are three sheep running, and Kokopelli—he turns up everywhere.

Always he is shown as being humpbacked and playing a flute. They say he came out of the earth as a grasshopper and turned up as our god of mischief. The losing, or breaking, or mislaying of things, and all the other troubles known to humans can be blamed on Kokopelli." He handed it back. "Only our people carve like that. You're lucky to have such a flute."

"I got it from the man at the trading place. I gave him the basket that Mother made for me," said the boy. "He liked it, and after we'd traded, he showed it to some of the other traders."

"Everyone likes your mother's baskets."

Since daybreak they had been traveling, climbing up through the broken canyon wall, away from the river where they had spent two days at the trading place. Both carried packs, and the old man labored up the trail under his heavy load. The boy seemed to carry his with ease. He was a small brown boy of maybe eleven winters. His wild black hair had been cut, but not lately, leaving bangs above his dark eyes. And, like all the people of his tribe, all the fat had been stripped from him by the desert sun, leaving him lean and quick like the gray coyote—and you knew just by looking at him that he could run long and fast, like the coyote runs. You noticed his eyes first, dark brown with a sharp crinkly spark about them—and he looked at you straight on, as if there was nothing hidden about him. He was truly a boy of the desert and the beautiful land around him.

After reaching the top, they had walked through the tall trees to a spring with a small running stream. Here they sat, resting and eating some of the food they carried in their packs.

"If you're about to blow that thing, do it softly," said the grandfather. "I'm tired. Climbing cliffs should be only for the very young. I'd like to rest a little before going on." He lay back, closing his eyes.

The boy fingered the flute, searching for notes, and he blew softly like the old man said. From across the small stream there came answering sounds—small mewing sounds—and a black bear, very young and scared and skinny, came into the clearing, stopped short at the boy's feet, and sat there sniffing. Reaching out his hands, the boy touched the small thing's head, and sensing no harm, the bear warmed to him and came closer, and was soon clutched tightly in the boy's arms.

The old man sat up and watched as the boy and the bear looked at and touched and made small sounds to each other. Finally he said, "This is bear country up here on the canyon rim. They like the aspens and pines. They can't live in the canyons and deserts lower down because it's too hot for them. Somewhere there is a mother searching for her cub, and it would not be well if she should find us."

"He's lost, Grandfather. I know he is. No one could be afraid of anything so skinny and scared—even if he is a bear. You can tell he's hungry. Here, bear, eat some of this." He took some bits of meat from his pack. "Look at him eat! Can I keep him, Grandfather?"

"We can take him with us, but only your mother can let you keep him. We should go now, or it will be dark when we come to the village. Can you carry the bear, or shall I?"

"He won't be heavy, Grandfather. He can ride on my shoulder."

It was the time of early spring upon the land. At the stream the catkins still clung to the willows and the aspen trees, and the grass was greening at the edges of the water. This was high country, this place of trees and running water. The trees thinned as the boy and the old man dropped down toward the desert. They could see before them the far reaches of the land, broken with canyons and gullies, flat buttes, and lovely pinnacles. It was red rock country, with blue mountains to the north and west. Above was the great arch of sky with white clouds that cast crooked shadows across the broken land.

And they walked, the old man with the tired legs and the boy, carrying presents on their backs, and bringing with them a small black bear. Moving toward the west, they left behind the high country; it was warmer here and they could smell the clean scent of the sage, and the juniper, and the piñon pine. To pass time while walking, the old man asked the boy, "Could you tell the people of our tribes from all the others at the trading place?"

"I think so. Our people looked and talked like us. All the others were different. I guess the way they dressed and wore their hair made them so."

"That's right. Did you notice the two men with the shells and the salt?"

"Yes. They had long stringy hair, their coverings were torn and dirty, and they talked funny."

"That is so. They were people from the west. They come very far, across many mountains and deserts, and live by a big water. And, son, don't ever say someone talks funny. They talk different from you, that's all.

"Could you tell the men from the plains country to the east

and north?"

"I think so. Were they the ones with the painted faces, the braided hair, the eagle feathers, and the fancy moccasins? One, I remember, had a necklace of bear claws. They came trading soft robes of animal skins, and clothing covered with designs made from the quills of porcupines."

"This is so," said the old man. "If you go far enough to the east and north, you will come to where these people live. You will see great herds of the animals they call bison. There are so many at times that the plains are black with them—as many as we have rocks in our rivers.

"At the traders' there were men from one other place—a place far to the south across many canyons and rivers. If you walked maybe two changes of the moon, you would come to their country. You saw them, with their large curved noses, and earrings that pulled their ears down nearly to their shoulders. These earrings are made from a heavy yellow stuff that shines when it is worked into jewelry. I know where there is a whole layer of it back in the Blue Mountains. Someday I'll learn how they do it. And you saw the clothes they wore in many bright colors. Did you see the feathers they brought? Bright green and red feathers from birds that live in dense forests. Cloth and corn and beads they brought with them. They are rich and live in fine houses. Also, they are a mean people, sometimes coming at night to steal our young girls and young men. They carry them to their country where they are kept as slaves. On certain days slaves are brought to a great temple where the slaves' living hearts are torn from their bodies and offered to the Sun God.

"The plains people also steal our young sons and daughters to become slaves, and the slaves do the hard labor in their villages. The men who do the stealing, both from the plains and from the far south, our tribes call the Wolf Men, and you must always be careful, because you never know when they are about.

"Our own people are different. If a person from one of our tribes harms another or steals anything, that person is brought before the elders and sometimes driven from the tribe.

"If a young man of our people wants to marry, he will seek out a girl, preferably from another village. It's best this way—it brings new blood to the villages. He will meet her at the Harvest Dance, or any event where many come together. Maybe he will give her a present or come to see her at her own village. If they like each other well enough, he will ask her parents if they will accept him as a son. Then the parents of both boy and girl get together for a marriage ceremony and a huge celebration that sometimes lasts for days. There is much singing and dancing and beating on the big drum.

"The young people almost always come to live in the village of the girl. My son and his wife, your mother and father, lived for a time with her people. Then, when your grandmother died, they came to our village to live and to take care of me. Your father's death was very hard on your mother, but she stayed here with me. I'm sure she thinks of me as her father, and I think of her as my own blood daughter."

The afternoon was upon them. They left tracks in the warm sand that showed they'd passed on tough, bare feet. Where the sand was soft, the tracks sunk deep because of the heavy packs they carried.

Once on the trail, while resting in the shade of a lone juniper, the boy looked at the old man, who seemed to be studying something in the far distance, or trying to bring some thought to his lips. "Is anything wrong?" he asked. "You seem sad."

He got no answer until the old man was ready. Finally he spoke. "Somewhere inside me I carry two memories that are like stones. Sometimes I take these stones and hold them in my hand. The one is of your grandmother. How lovely she was when she was young. Her eyes were always upon me, and she was soft to touch, and the bread she made was wonderful. The other stone is of your father, who was my son. Somehow you remind me of him. Maybe it's the way you talk or walk, or the way you sometimes look at me."

"I don't remember much about him," said the boy. "I was pretty young when he left. But I do remember his laughing, and the way he would catch me when I ran to him, and how he'd throw me up to his shoulder."

"He was a good man, and a great hunter."

"He made me a spear once. I still have it, and keep it with my things."

"No one knew animals as well as Hawk Man, your father. It was almost as if he could see each living thing from high in the air. After he killed with his spear, he would sit beside the dead animal and talk to it, thanking it for the life it gave, and telling it that its death was necessary to keep food in the village. He was a good man."

As they talked, the small bear climbed into the boy's lap and

reached with its red tongue to lick his face, and the boy and the bear hugged. The old man laughed. "Some hunter you'll be," he said. "Every live thing will be carried home to be loved by you and fed by your mother. No, you'll never be a hunter like your father."

"Tell me again how my father died."

The old man sat and stared into the distance, trying to think how best to say it. Finally he spoke. "It was a day in spring. He and Broken Stick, your friend's father, took their spears and a basket of food into the ledges of the Red River Canyon. They went to hunt the curved-horn sheep that live there through the winter. While they were hunting in the cliffs, they were separated by a late spring blizzard. Broken Stick searched for days, trying to find your father. A search party was also sent out, but Hawk Man was never found."

They traveled on, the old man, the boy, and the small black bear held in the boy's young arms. Near sunset they came to the bare fields where their people planted corn and squash each spring. These things, picked in the late summer or fall, fed the people each year through the long winter.

"A few more warm days now and the women will be up here with their digging sticks," said the old man. "It's almost time for the planting again, and time for our dancing. I can feel it—almost smell it in the air."

"How can you tell when it's time?" asked the boy.

"When the moon and the wind are right, when the grass shows green, and when the bite has gone from the night air, then we know it's time for the dances."

"Can I come and watch?"

"If you sit quietly back in the shadows. I'll know you're there. Only the elders can take part in the planting ceremony. We must be very careful to do it exactly as our fathers have taught us so the planting and the harvest will be good."

Soon they came to the canyon, and they could smell smoke from the cook fires in the village. Moving backward and down on wooden ladders, and clutching the handholds cut in the hard rock face of the cliff, they worked their way to the canyon floor. Rounding a turn and up two more ladders, they were at the village.

The old man was always happy when coming home. The huge cave high above the canyon floor was like a large, friendly cupped hand protecting the many stone buildings of the village. They were rooms, really, squeezed close together—some on top of others, the flat roofs of the lower rooms serving as porches or front yards for those on top. The upper rooms were reached by wooden ladders. Among the people were skilled masons who built straight walls of fitted stone held together with clay mortar. They left openings for windows and low doorways, which were covered at times with animal hides to keep out wind and weather. It was a noisy place, housing perhaps fifteen families. Children played on the walkways between and around the houses. There were stacks of wood for cooking fires, and as they climbed the ladder the old man looked up and saw the smoke rise, as it had for many years, to blacken the upper reaches of the cave. They heard a dog bark, a woman calling, and somewhere a small baby crying.

"I'll be glad to see my bed again," said the grandfather. "Sleeping on the ground among the rocks is fit only for the young." The best part of every trip was coming home. The grandfather had first seen the two rock rooms when he came to the village to live with his new bride and her parents. Her people had lived there for many generations. His son had been born there, and his wife had died there. And his son, Hawk Man, had brought his own young wife there to care and cook for the old man. All living and sleeping were done in the one front room; the other was used for storage. When the son's children were born, he talked with the old man and they built two rooms on top for the new family. Things changed with the death of Hawk Man. Mother and daughter now stayed in the two upper rooms, and the young son, Cricket, moved downstairs with his grandfather.

The two rooms on the lower floor were some of the oldest in the village. The walls were straight and built solidly with worked stone. The roof was framed with stout pine rafters brought from the Far Blue Mountains. Laid crossways over the rafters were willows from the canyon. Corn shucks laid on the willows and clay on the shucks formed the ceiling, which was also the floor of the two rooms above.

One had to stoop low to enter the door to the grandfather's room. On the floor along the sidewalls were beds. Logs were laid the long way with the room and an arm's length out from the wall. The space between log and wall was filled with dried corn shucks. Soft hides, and blankets made of woven rabbit hair and turkey feathers, served as coverings. The two beds also were the room's seating. On the boy's side, near the door, the mother kept her large jug filled with fresh water and a few pots she used for cooking, which she did just outside the doorway.

Things hung on the walls from pegs driven into the clay mortar between the rock surfaces. On the boy's side was the spear his father had made and given to him, along with a small bow and some arrows. The grandfather's side was quite festive, hung with *kachina* figures carved from the roots of cottonwood trees and covered with paint and fur and feathers. Here was where he kept spare walking sticks and some of the things he used with his singing. At the far wall was another low door that led to the old man's storeroom, and over the door hung a beautiful carved wooden mask of a thunderbird, which the old man had used as a young boy back in his own village.

Now he was home again. He raised the hide covering the door and entered with his heavy pack, followed by his grandson. On the grandson's bed sat the mother and sister, their faces lighted by the flickering flames from a small oil lamp.

"We were expecting you," said the mother. "A small boy saw you come down off the cliff and came to tell me. I've already fixed cold rabbit and some of the bread I made this morning. I know you're hungry."

Said the old man, "It will be good."

"I see you've brought me a small bear, son. I hope he's good for eating."

"He was lost and scared, Mother. Can I keep him? I'll take good care of him."

"Like you took care of the coyote puppy that the dogs killed? Or the horned toads? Or the hawk with the broken wing? Do

you remember the snake that was loose in the house for days?"

"Will you let me keep him?"

"Eat now. Tomorrow we'll decide. I must sleep before I can give you an answer."

"Here, Snow Flower. Hold him for me. He won't bite if you pat his forehead," and he handed the squirming bear to his sister.

"The trading was good, and we brought many things," said the old man. "Maybe we should wait until morning when we're not so tired to open the packs."

"See, Mother, he likes me," said the girl. "He's sucking my fingers."

"It's good to be home," said the old man.

Chapter
TWO

Morning came, and the mother sat on her heels, kneading and shaping corn dough with her hands. A small fire, mostly red coals, cast a glow upon her and on the rock face of the house behind her. The boy, clutching the small bear, came through the doorway and sat beside her.

"You slept well?" asked the woman.

"It was good to be in my own bed," answered the boy.

"And the trading? Did you like the trading?"

"There were people from all over, and they brought many

things—things I'd never seen or even dreamed about. Yes, I liked the trading and would like to go again next year." This is what he said, but his thoughts were on the bear. Would she let him keep it? I'll let her speak about it first, he thought.

Snow Flower came from the house and sat. "May I hold him?" she asked. "He's so soft, and I think he likes me." She took the bear in her arms.

Then the old man came, carrying the two packs. He set them down and held his hands before the fire. "You make fine bread," he said. "The smell of it woke me. I keep thinking that it's good to be home."

Now that his hands were warm, he set his old fingers to untying the stiff knots in the cord that bound the packs. "They liked your baskets at the trading place, Basket Woman, and we brought back many things. Here, look at this—blue corn. I'd never seen blue corn in all my life. We ate blue bread at the traders'. What did you think, Cricket? Was it good?"

"It was very good."

"It comes from the far south, beyond the two red rivers."

"We'll plant it," said the woman, "and surprise our friends here in the village."

"Here's salt," said the old man, "and a piece of cloth. Cloth is woven from the fibers of a plant called cotton. This piece is white, but we saw it in many colors. Feel it. Feel how soft it is. I got it big enough to wrap around your middle."

"It's very soft," said the woman. "My friends won't know me."

"Snow Flower, these are for you. Here are some cloth and some shells for your ears. These came from the big water far to the west. And these—beads of turquoise stone with small holes already drilled to make a necklace."

"You bring good things," said Basket Woman. "Now what did you bring for yourself?"

"A black robe. It's heavy and fills one whole pack. Maybe it will keep me warm next winter. Here, feel how thick and heavy it is. It is the finished hide of an animal that comes from the east and north where the plains people live. One man drew me a picture of it. It was huge. You can tell by the size of the hide. The head was rounded, with horns that curved up, and it had a beard. It was a strange and wondrous thing even to think about. The animal is called the bison. One day I hope to see one."

"And you, my son. Besides the bear, what did you bring for yourself?"

"I heard them play music, Mother, when the old men sat at the fire in the evening. The sounds they made were beautiful—like no sounds I'd ever heard. It's a flute, Mother. Grandfather said it was made by our people. One day, when I learn how, I'll play for you."

"You're very good to me, and I know you've been waiting—waiting to talk about the bear. Now, my son, Cricket." She always called him by his name when things were important. "Cricket, you can keep the bear, I guess, but he can't stay in the house with us. If he stays outside, the dogs will kill him. So think how you will care for him."

It was here the old man spoke. "As you know, son, everyone in this village belongs to the Bear Clan. The tracks carved in the rock by the ladders are bear tracks, and people know who we are by these signs. I will speak to the old men, and I am sure they will welcome your bear. When you've finished here, go find your friend Sheep, and we'll make a home for your bear. At the back of the cave, near where we keep the turkeys, there is a place. We'll build it of rocks like a little house. This morning we shall plan it."

Cricket's good friend, the son of Broken Stick and Gray Mouse, lived next door. When he was very small, they called him Sheep's Child, but as he grew, the "Child" part got whittled away by his mother to just plain "Sheep." The boy was very quick, and some-times before she could get the two words from her mouth, the boy was gone. The only time either she or the father ever used "Sheep's Child" was when they were angry and had him pinned to the wall with their eyes. Broken Stick had been the hunting part-ner of Hawk Man, Cricket's father, and since the father's death, he treated Cricket as a second son. The two boys were within days of being the same age, and they played and laughed and wrestled like twins. Each treated the other's home and property as if they were his own. When Sheep first spied the bear, he became very excited. "Will they let you keep him?" he cried. "If they do, it will be a good summer!"

"I can keep him," said Cricket, "but he can't stay in the house with us. Grandfather said we could build him his own place down by the turkeys. You can help if you want."

So they built the bear's house—built it of flat rocks the boys carried from the ledges in the canyon, and the clay they dug from a place near the spring. The old man formed the walls from floor to ceiling at the back of the cave near where the turkeys lived.

"We'll need a door," he said. "Bring me some straight pieces of cedar the size of your arms." He formed a door of cedar bars where people could look in and the bear could look out when it was shut, and he tied it together with rawhide wrappings. He did it cleverly so the bear couldn't chew on it from the inside. "It's finished now...except for two things."

"What's that?"

"Get baskets of cedar bark so your bear will have a soft bed."

"What else?"

"Bring the bear," the old man said.

The bear was brought, and Cricket said, "Hey, bear! You heard what Mother said. You be good now, or I'll put you in with the turkeys."

At first the bear didn't care much for his new home. He whined when the boys left. From their cages, the turkeys inspected their new neighbor with strange gurgling noises. Soon, though, everything settled down, and the bear went to sleep, and the turkeys went back to scratching in the sand.

The grandfather was a small, tough man with white hair tied in a bun that rode his shoulders. When he smiled, he showed teeth worn flat almost to the gums from having eaten the meal made from corn ground on the stone *metate*—and he smiled often, for he was a happy man. His black eyes, still full of light and sparkle, shone from a wrinkled face. In fact, he was wrinkled all over, like an old deer hide left too long near a fire. A large rabbit skin forming a breechcloth was his only clothing in summer. Wintertime found him with a robe of coyote or badger hides. Sometimes,

when there was snow, he wore furs wrapped around his feet and ankles. At all other times, his feet were bare.

One of five elders in the village, he was a maker of pictures, a collector and dispenser of herbs and wisdom. Most of his time was spent collecting things, such as leaves and bark and roots from the desert plants. These he used when the villagers came to him in sickness, and he knew the songs to sing and the hand motions to make at every visit. He collected sand and clay and bits of earth of many colors to use when painting, and his collecting took him on long journeys. Many days were spent looking for things he needed for his work. He visited special places for different things. Once he found blue-green copper stones and bloodred iron earth side by side under a ledge in the Far Blue Mountains, and he found sulfur, dried and very yellow, near a hot spring in the desert. A dry lake gave him sand white as salt. All these things, when ground up fine, made wondrous colors for his sand paintings.

This old man was much loved by his people. They called him Song Maker because he knew the songs of tending and healing the sick, and he knew all the chants to sing to the gods on special occasions. From old men he had learned the songs of his people's past wanderings in the desert, and how they were to live in harmony with things that lived and were close around them. He knew all the songs to all the gods who governed the things around them. It was said that he could coax water from even the smallest of clouds at the rain dances.

Once, though, his name had been Runner. As a young man, he was faster than anyone in the village, but now his bones were old and brittle, and his wind came in gasps when running. Now he was called Song Maker.

Off to one side of the village, still under the arch of the cliff, there was a place set aside for the old men. Most villages had a kiva, a special room, for this purpose, but here there was a place for a fire, a cleared space for dancing, and a small building to hold their ceremonial things. This was the old men's place, and no one came here uninvited.

Once there had been a kiva here, built by the great-great-grandfathers of these old men. A kiva is a large round room, used for ceremonies, built underground—impossible on the floor within the cave, for it was solid rock. The old men built it up from the canyon floor with cut stone like the houses, built it level with the floor of the cave. One could walk out onto its flat roof, with its square opening and ladder, from the floor of the cave. In the second year, the floods came and washed the kiva down the canyon. It was rebuilt, and the same thing happened again. It was decided then to forget the kiva and set aside a place within the cave—a place for the old men.

Early next morning, after helping the boys with the bear house, the grandfather was kneeling in this open space with his bags of colors spread before him. He took sand in his right hand and let it filter through his fingers to form a skin-flat figure on the rock floor. A large Corn Mother and a smaller Squash Mother lay before him in many colors. And the old men shook the gourd rattles and fingered the big drum while the grandfather sang the planting song that had been handed down by old men long since gone:

Let your spirit be with us,
Corn Mother,
Share with us the corn
From last year's planting.
And let it be with our women
As they prepare the earth
And our old men
Planting new seeds
For the coming season.
And let the new plants
Come from the earth
Strong and green,
Corn Mother,
And let the rain come,
And the small wind come,
And let the new corn be good.

Each of the old men took ground cornmeal and seeds of the squash and, in turn, made their offerings to the Corn Mother and to the Squash Mother, then returned to their drum and rattles.

When evening came, the painting was gone. Hugging the bear, Cricket sat in the shadows watching the five old men and watching the flames of a large fire jump and dance, lending life to the darkness and to the Place of the Old Men.

Whenever the bear moved or grew restless, the boy soothed him.

"How're you going to learn about these things if you wiggle so? Be still and watch and listen." And the bear looked at him and was still.

The drums and the singing were exciting to the boy, but the bear slept. Only when there was dancing did the bear come alive as he jumped in time to the beating of the drums. Far into the night it went before the party was over, and the old men said that it went very well. Morning found the place deserted, except for the boy and the small black bear sleeping in each other's arms.

Chapter
THREE

The bite of winter had left the land, and the two boys played with the bear. They taught him to climb the ladders and use the handholds to go up and down the cliff's steep face. They ran with him, talked to him, and even wrestled with him. And the bear became a part of them—a part of their play and the things they did.

"He's wonderful!" cried Sheep. "I wish he was mine."

Cricket's mother took this time to climb to the flat country above the canyon with her digging sticks, and to prepare the

33

earth for the blue and the yellow corn, and the squash the grandfather would plant. She made her rows straight, and she used the land allotted to her by the old men of the village. Looking all around when she was finished, she was pleased.

The days went by, and the young plants showed their green leaves in the new-dug earth. Then one evening after the meal, the mother spoke. "Cricket, my son, your playing days are over for a while. Tonight you will start watching at the fields. You will be up there until I come to bring you home. Take your bear with you, and your new flute. Maybe while you practice playing, you will scare away the birds."

They took with them a jug of water, a small bit of dried meat, and two hairy skins to keep him warm and to protect him from the morning dew, and they climbed the cliff face to the planted fields.

"I've seen the quail go down a row and eat every tender shoot of corn," the mother said, "and I've seen the rabbits sit and nibble at everything that's green and growing. They will come mostly in the early morning just when it's getting light, so plan to be awake and watching. I know you can holler really loud, so holler when it's needed." She left him seated in the field, and the night closed in around him.

Nighttime can be long, dark, scary, even wonderful, and the boy felt all these things. He watched the stars appear and fill the sky with brightness almost like moonlight. Some animal as large as a coyote or a badger—it could have been a ghost—came sniffing. The bear whined and snuggled in the boy's arms. Cricket slept and knew it was morning when he heard the cock

quail calling. There were three sharp little notes beyond the field in the low brush. . .and he saw the quail come. The small, pert hen was leading the flock with quick, short steps, while the cock watched from his perch on a dead limb of a low-growing cedar, calling directions as the head man should. There they were, the whole flock heading down the corn rows. Cricket stood quick and tall and shouted, "Hooo-ha!" and the quail lifted with exploding wings. Then he saw it—saw the rabbit with the white bobbing tail, leaping down the field, and the boy hollered again, "Hooo-ha!" and the rabbit was long gone. Next there was the black crow with cold dark eyes that lifted its wings and found a perch on a tall red rock. A whirling stick sent it soaring out over the deep canyon, leaving behind only its angry cries.

Sunrise brought the fields to life. Other children, doing their time in the fields, hollered at each other and stood tall while dodging the sticks and rocks thrown by their playful friends. To children who lived pressed in by canyon walls, this rolling flat country was new and wonderful. The high arch of the sky and the vast distances stirred in them a great new feeling, a feeling almost like a snake shedding a too-tight skin, and they ran and tumbled and pointed to the Far Blue Mountains. No bird or rabbit moved with all the racket stirring. Three young girls with wreaths of white yucca blossoms in their hair strayed to the canyon's edge. Looking down, they screamed in fright at the dizzy drop to the rocky bottom far below, then turned away and ran back to the flat safety of the cornfields.

Now the mothers came, bringing food and jugs of fresh water. They sat with the children and talked with them and were pleased with the way the new plants grew. "See how green it is," they said, "and see the way the leaves unfurl—one from the other."

Cricket's mother was there early with enough water and food for both the boy and the bear. She sat with Cricket while the bear played around their feet. "Is he behaving himself?" she asked.

"He's been good, Mother. He even chased a bird. And the kids like him. They're here playing with him all the time."

"Well, keep them off the new plants. Sometimes children can be worse than quail or rabbits." When she was gone, Sheep came from the next patch and the boys sat a while, then tumbled with the bear. "This will be a wonderful time," thought Cricket.

In the afternoon he looked at the new flute. Besides being made of bone and carved with figures, it fit easily in his hands. At one end there was a place for blowing, and there were holes along the top—each hole for a finger, and the thumbs were for holding along the bottom. He remembered how the old men played their flutes, and he remembered the wild, wonderful music.

Now he carefully brought the flute to his lips. The first scruffy noise was awful, more like the lonesome howlings of a lost coyote puppy than music. The weird sounds sent the bear scrambling down through the rows of corn and brought Sheep running. "It makes a great racket," he said. "Someday will you let me blow it?"

By the time the sun was far down in the western sky, his fingers had discovered the holes—the right holes for the notes from high to low and back to high again. By the time the stars were showing, he could hum a simple tune, then play the same sounds on the flute. Sheep was long gone, and the bear, who had disappeared with the first notes, came back and curled up on the sheepskins at his feet. Cricket reached down with his hand and scratched at the bear's back. "Hey, Bear! Next year, you'll be bigger than I am. You won't need to chase the birds— just stand up and growl. You'll scare 'em then, won't you?"

As the days in the fields slipped by, the two boys sat, mostly talking or playing with the bear. One day when he'd earned it, they would give the bear a name. Now he was simply Bear. It mattered little to him what his name was. In fact, he didn't even know he was a bear. He thought he was a hairy boy, and did all the things the boys did. He could rear up and walk on two legs like a boy. Sometimes, though, when running, he slipped back to four. Then he could run faster than the boys. He was a better wrestler, too. When he tried to talk, though, he had trouble, and the sounds came out more like whining or crying. And the boys loved him, and wrestled with him, and ran with him until all three were tired.

There was an evening when a storm came. They could see it first, far to the west over the canyon. It started with the junipers dancing in the high wind that swept eye-stinging sand across the fields. The clouds closed in all around them, making it dark as night. The first drops of rain fell and stirred the dust in small explosions, and the wind stopped, and suddenly it was very cold. Coming now in earnest, sheets of water drenched the land, and the children huddled beneath the low juniper trees, holding hides and baskets over their heads, warding off the rain. All night they waited for the storm to lift, and they were tired and wet when morning brought sunshine breaking through the clouds. Morning also brought the mothers with food and jugs of fresh water. They examined first the children, then the corn and squash plants. Everything was very wet, but good.

The tribe's two hunters, Broken Stick and Tracker Man, came one day and sat in the shade with the two boys and the bear. Broken Stick was Sheep's father. "We miss you since you came up here," he said. "Maybe not you, but the racket you make. The village is not the same without you. How about a drink? We've come all the way from the Far Blue Mountains since morning."

They were thirsty and tired, they said, and their hunt had gone sour when they lost the deer they'd followed since early dawn. "Maybe we should take the bear" said Tracker Man. "At least he's got some fat on him and would make a dinner for someone."

"Better keep your eye on him, Cricket," said Broken Stick.

"Who? The bear or Tracker?"

The hunter chuckled. "You're like your father. He could make me laugh just by the way he talked."

"I remember when I was very small," said Cricket, "you came running to the village one day. You and Father had chased some deer into a box canyon and had them trapped there. I remember everyone running to the place. We formed a line, and hollered, and waved our arms to keep the deer from running. Then you and Father killed them with your spears. What I remember most, though, was the fright in the deers' eyes as they lay dying. . .and all the blood. I remember how excited the people were when we carried the meat back to the village. I think I was sick when I saw the blood."

"I guess you'll make a better flute player than a hunter," said Broken Stick. "Blood and hunting go together. Your father was one of the best hunters I ever knew, and I miss him. I must go now."

Every morning an old woman left the village and slowly climbed the cliff's face, using the handholds and the ladders. Her gray hair hung about her wrinkled face, and she moved slowly, like the very old, rather hesitant and limping painfully. She was bent forward, so that as she walked she appeared always to be searching for something on the ground. Cricket's grandfather had told him once that as far back as he could remember the old woman had looked this way—always old and bent, with gray hair.

As often as she passed through the fields where the children watched, she never looked at them and never spoke. She moved toward the rolling hills where the piñons and the junipers grew. This was high desert, and the trees had spaced themselves far apart so their roots could absorb what moisture the hot skies offered, and they grew low and were twisted by the wind. They were old trees. Some had seen hundreds of winters and had scattered many dead limbs upon the ground.

The woman gathered this dead wood, sometimes tying it in bundles to carry on her back. The larger limbs she dragged behind her, always heading for the same spot on the canyon rim. Here she stopped and looked down, then hollered in a high thin voice that echoed among the cliffs, "Hooo-ha! Watch yourselves. I now throw the wood." She threw it far out above the canyon, where it dropped—sometimes it seemed forever, falling to the rocks below with a splintering crash. Hearing this, she seemed satisfied that all was well, and turned toward the rolling hills for another load. The people in the village called her Wood Woman.

One day the two boys watched her throw the wood. They waited until she was safely gone, then they took the bear and went to her spot on the canyon rim. Looking down, they sucked in their breath at the long drop to the rocks below.

"It's a long way down," said Sheep. "How far do you think it is?"

"Too far to jump," said Cricket. "If I threw a rock, I'll bet I could count all my fingers twice before it hit the bottom."

"You throw and I'll count." A rock was thrown. It was so far down they couldn't even hear it hit bottom.

They found a stick, but before throwing it, Cricket hollered, "I am Wood Woman. Watch yourselves. I now throw the wood." Off it went, then more sticks. "Hooo-ha!" they hollered. By now they were almost marching—out to find sticks, then back to the rim for throwing. The bear followed, sometimes boylike on hind legs, more waddling than marching. There was much laughing and hollering, "Hooo-ha!" Bending over and limping, they walked like the old woman, and they laughed until they were tired of it all and went back to the cornfields.

"That was fun," said Cricket. "Let's do it again tomorrow."

Next morning, shortly after sunup, Cricket's sister, Snow Flower, came, bringing with her the girl Yellow Leaf, who was a cousin of Sheep. "Grandfather wants you both to come to the village," she told the boys. "You are to leave the bear with us, and we're to watch the fields until you get back. Don't worry about anything here." The boys headed for the canyon and home.

When they found the grandfather in the old men's part of the village, he wasn't smiling. "Sit here and listen," he said. Five old men sat at the big drum. Two were beating a low, quiet rhythm, and all five were chanting in high voices. This went on for some time, and the boys, after sitting and listening, squirmed on the hard rock seats.

Finally the grandfather spoke. "You two are in great trouble. Yesterday you made fun of an old woman who works very hard. Look around you, and if you look closely, you will see that everyone here keeps busy at the things he or she does best for the good of the village. This old woman hauls wood for the use of all the people. What would it be like if, at every meal, your mother had to search for wood to cook? Even though she is old and crippled, the Wood Woman never complains, and the people see that she is fed and has warm robes in the winter. We take care of her in all things.

"So, my young friends, we shall see if it is funny. Tomorrow and the next day the old woman will stay here and rest while

you two do the work she does. For two days you shall haul the
wood and throw it into the canyon. Never in those two days
shall you sit and rest, and there will be no complaining. So go
now and be careful of the snakes."

Gathering the wood was hot, thirsty work. Although half the
trees in the high country were very old, they were small and
twisted and gave very little shade. The rocks scattered about
were sharp and drew the sun to them, and the heat held low to
the ground. Bare feet, though tough, could not tolerate the sharp
thorns of low-growing cactus, and the boys were careful where
they stepped. And there were rattlesnakes, as the old man had
said, lying in some of the shady places, coiled and mean when
disturbed. From up here the boys could see very much of their
known world, and it was a huge world that seemed to go forever
in four directions. The sky, like a great blue dome splashed with
puffs of clouds, held everything in place, including the heat that
bore down upon them. They worked at tearing dead limbs from
old trees, and they picked up the sharp, dry pieces that lay scattered on the ground. Having gathered enough to make a load
for each one, they went down through the rocks and brush to
the canyon rim. "Hooo-ha! Watch yourselves—we now throw
the wood!" On each trip, they stopped at the fields to get water
from their friends.

The boys struggled for two days under the hot sun, and when
they were finished, they stood before the old men of the village.
"You have done well, and we hope you have learned from this.

Go to your homes tonight, and tomorrow return to the fields. You may go now."

At first light next morning, the boys climbed the cliff's face to the fields above. They found the bear, who stood on the sheepskins lonesome and whining. Snow Flower was nowhere to be seen. Yellow Leaf had sat with her the night before and thought she was here with the bear. They waited, and the sun moved high in the sky.

While Cricket stayed by the sheepskins, other children scattered through the fields, searching. No one had seen his sister, and he grew worried. "Sheep, stay here with the bear and watch while I go down to the village. I should tell my mother and grandfather." The bear whined when he left, but Sheep rubbed his head and soothed him.

It seemed to Cricket that it took forever to get back to the village. "Mother!" he hollered as he came chugging up to their door. "We can't find Snow Flower. We've looked everywhere in the fields. Did she come back here to the village?"

"I haven't seen her. Grandfather, have you seen Snow Flower?" The people came running to see what had happened.

Later in the afternoon, the family stood in the fields where most of the people of the village had gathered. Broken Stick and Tracker Man had just returned from a long search they'd made through the wild brush land. Broken Stick spoke. "We found no sign of her, but we did see tracks. At this time of year, all of our people are barefoot. The tracks we found were made by two men wearing moccasins. They were fresh and were headed east toward the Far Blue Mountains. We will follow these tracks just to see whether or not she is with them. These people would make her a slave."

Chapter
FOUR

A t first no one wanted to believe it. Kidnapped! Little Snow Flower kidnapped! Broken Stick and Tracker Man were back at the place of the moccasin tracks. "They're moving fast," said Tracker. "Let's follow along and see if there's any sign of the girl."

At the fields most of the people had left for the village, leaving behind the children who still had to watch the growing things. "Sheep, watch for me," said Cricket. "I want to see if my mother is all right. She was very upset when she left here. I'll be back soon."

Even as he climbed down the ladder to the village, he could hear the high wailing of the women. There sat his mother and all the mothers in front of his home. Just as when someone had died, they sat there rocking back and forth and weeping, tearing at their hair and making bloody gashes in their bodies. Cricket tried speaking to his mother, but she paid no attention. At the place of the old men, he found his grandfather, who was singing to the rhythm of a small drum he was stroking with his fingers. A song for Snow Flower—one he was making from his own thoughts, singing to the rhythm of the drum:

> You were newborn
> When I held you in one hand
> And touched you
> With the other,
> You looked at me
> With dark eyes
> And you grasped my thumb
> And smiled at me.
> My heart swelled then,
> And swelled when
> We laughed together
> As you were growing.
> Now your dark eyes
> Are gone from me,
> And your laughter
> Is gone from me,
> And my heart swells
> And there is no more laughter.

Not even speaking, Cricket returned to the house and the wailing sounds of the women. From his room he took the spear his father had made for him, and in passing took some dried meat from where his mother stored it. He wrapped it in a piece of hide and looked for a small clay jug that might hold water. Walking past the women, he climbed down the ladder and headed for the fields.

"Sheep," he said, "losing Snow Flower to the kidnappers was my fault. If we hadn't played at being the Wood Woman, she would still be at home, and we would have watched the fields. I've got my spear, I've got my food and water, and I'm going to see if I can find her, even if I have to go over the Far Blue Mountains. Would you come with me?"

"What about watching the fields?"

"We'll get some of the kids. They'll do it. They'll watch if I leave my flute for them to play with."

"What about your grandfather and your mother—did you tell them you were leaving?"

"I tried, but they weren't listening."

So they went—two boys carrying a pack of food, a jug of water, and a short spear, followed by a small black bear. Up through the fields, up through the old forest where they'd gathered wood they went, their faces pointed toward the Far Blue Mountains.

It was high desert country they traveled. They passed lovely buttes and standing rocks, and they crossed gullies where flood waters had torn all living things from the earth. There were great areas of red rocks, and sand where sage and juniper and black brush grew. These places were at their best, showing spring flowers and cactus blooming. Prickly pear, barrel cactus, and a small, low-growing, very stickery thing that almost jumped at those passing—all were in beautiful, waxlike bloom. And the yucca, the wonderful yucca plants whose straight-standing shafts were a cascade of small, bell-shaped pearly flowers. Scarlet paintbrush, sego lilies (the yellow kind), and desert mallow peppered the earth before them. In tall patches grew the yellow beeweed, and against the cliffs on the sunny side was the wonderfully beautiful poisoned leaf jimsonweed with white lily flowers as big as a tall man's fist.

Along the way were long stretches of slickrock—places where nothing grew—that were smooth and easy on bare feet. There they found several holes with stale water where bugs lived and moved about when they lay on their bellies to drink.

Once when the sun was still high, they came to a canyon that was not too far across, but very deep—almost as deep as the one that hid their own village. "We'll have to find a way to cross," said Cricket, and they walked, looking until they found where the edge of a cliff had torn loose and fallen, scattering huge boulders from the rim to the canyon floor. Down they went, feeling their way between, over, and around the rocks. Upon reaching the bottom, they found shade beside a cliff.

"Grandfather once told me that where you find cottonwood trees, you'll also find water." They found such a tree, with roots that spread wide and clutched each crevice in the sand and slickrock. This tree had stood before the wild floods that raced down the canyon at times; you could tell by the mud and sticks clinging to its lower branches. From a bank by the roots, water seeped to

form a brackish pool.

"If you find live bugs in the water, the water will be good enough to drink. That's something else my grandfather told me," said Cricket. They found bugs swimming and drank from the pool, saving the water in the jug they'd brought from home.

"Look," said Sheep. "Look at the tracks." There were man tracks, both barefooted and with moccasins, but no small tracks that could have been made by a young girl.

"The plainsmen were here first," said Cricket. "They were followed by your father and Tracker Man. I think the men in the moccasins know something about Snow Flower. Maybe we can find out if we keep following them. They must be headed for the Far Blue Mountains—so let's find a way up the other side."

They walked the deep, shady bottom and poked their way into a small box canyon. Here they found that at one end, water had dug a deep wash coming in from the top. Working their way into this crevice, moving upward, but sometimes backtracking, they somehow made it to the top, where they found level ground.

The Far Blue Mountains seemed no closer as the boys hurried on. "Let's keep watching," said Cricket. "Maybe we'll see the men of the moccasins. They might lead us to Snow Flower."

All day, they worked their way over the rough country, sometimes broken with gullies and deep canyons—always moving east toward the mountains in the distance. Once, stopping in the shade of a low-growing juniper, they ate some of the food in the pack, and then trudged on again.

The sun was casting long shadows and was hanging very low behind them. "It will be dark soon. Maybe we should look for a place to spend the night," said Cricket. "I don't think we should be wandering in the dark." In a deep-cut wash, they found a small cave that had been formed in the side by storms and blowing sand. The boys, and even the bear, were very tired, and after eating some of their meat and drinking from the clay jug, they fell asleep.

At first light, they were awakened by the smell of wood smoke and cooking meat. Sheep poked Cricket and whispered, "It's the plainsmen! They're wearing moccasins and have feathers in their hair."

"We're in great trouble," said Cricket. "They know we're here and are waiting. Let's see if we can show them we're not scared. Try not to shake when they look at us. Let's see what happens." The boys and the bear came out from their cave and faced the strangers.

"No use running," said Sheep, and they stood watching.

The two men hardly looked up. There were no words spoken. A skinned rabbit on a stick was being held over a small cook fire. While it was still red and smoking, the men tore at it and ate. What was left was thrown to the boys and the bear, and while they picked at the bones, the men looked on.

The larger of the two men wore two feathers in his hair, and the other wore but one. They smelled of smoke and grease, and they had white and red paint smeared across their noses and under their eyes. Two Feathers moved around the boys and looked them over, then felt the bear as if judging him for fat. He spoke to One Feather, and in his own language he said, "The bear will follow the boys, so no need for tying him. We're almost out of food, so we'll kill and eat him this evening. If we kill him now, we must carry him, so let him walk. Walking meat, eh?" and he chuckled.

Of course, the boys didn't understand the words, but they read the hand motions and the eyes. Cricket knew exactly what the man had said and knew the bear was in great trouble.

Two Feathers then stood before Cricket and took the boy's spear. Taking a braided leather thong from a pack, he tied one end around Sheep's neck, the other end around Cricket's. He pulled and motioned them to move. Gathering up their gear and packs, the two feathered men motioned to the boys to do the same. They started walking, the boys being led by Two Feathers. One Feather followed, carrying Cricket's spear and one of his own. The bear, sensing things were wrong, came along behind, running free.

The feathered men set a fast pace, and they covered the rough country as if they were fearful of being followed. One Feather kept looking back, and the leader jerked at the rope if the boys lingered or stumbled. Towards afternoon, they came to a sink-hole with warm, stagnant water. Here they sat a while and drank. Two Feathers threw the boys some dried meat.

"Looks like someday soon we'll see the bison," said Cricket, trying to smile. Two Feathers, who seemed to be in charge, came at him and slapped him hard across the mouth. Then, by signs, he cupped the fingers of his left hand and from his own mouth seemed to be pulling words. With a flattened right hand, he chopped at the air between left hand and mouth. The meaning was very clear. NO talking!

Cricket was more surprised than hurt. No one had ever struck him before. No one. . . and he put his hand to his mouth and looked hard at the big man without smiling. Two Feathers motioned as if to hit again but backed away without touching him. One more drink and they again took the trail, same as before.

Since early morning, they had traveled through high desert country. The men, in moccasins, had kept to the hard and rocky parts of the trail. Cricket thought they did this to keep from leaving tracks. This was hard on bare feet, and his were cut in places and bleeding. His neck was sore from being jerked by the rawhide rope. Looking back, he saw that Sheep, too, was having the same trouble. The bear, being free, had chosen softer ground and seemed all right.

Near sunset, they came to higher ground—to the foothills of the Far Blue Mountains. The low junipers and piñons gave way to tall ponderosa pines that grew scattered and in small clumps. There were green meadows with knee-high grass, and at one place they saw mother elk with their calves in the distance, watching as they passed.

They came now to a trickle of a stream and a place of beaver dams and tall trees. Here they would spend the night. Knowing that the boys were tired, Two Feathers untied the cord that bound them and began gathering wood for a fire. He motioned for One Feather to bring the bear. The man was reaching for his knife when Cricket hollered and raised his hand. Both feathered men stopped what they were doing, and the boy pointed to his pack, then showed them the food he'd carried. Two Feathers examined the dried meat, looked at the bear, and decided on Cricket's

offering. We're safe until morning, Cricket thought. They think he's walking bear meat and that they can eat him anytime.

After they had eaten, the boys were bound again, and they curled up close together with the bear between them. The tall trees rustled in the wind, and the small fire crackled. Soon the two men lay back, and the camp was silent.

Sometime before morning, something stirred. There was shadowy movement near the sleeping men, and Cricket was awakened by thuds and a scuffling sound. Two shadowy figures rose and stood tall and dark against the starlit sky.

"Sheep! Cricket! Are you there?"

"We're here!"

The boys were soon untied, for the dark figures were Broken Stick and Tracker Man. "Bring your bear and come," one said, and the boys moved quickly.

Cricket ran back to where the two figures sprawled upon the ground by the dead fire. "Forgot my spear," he said.

"Keep close now," said Tracker. "We don't want to lose you in the dark."

They moved through the maze of trees and rocks with the dawn showing dimly at their backs. Always Tracker seemed to choose the easy way, and as they walked, Cricket spoke. "Did you kill them? Did you kill the two men? They were just lying there by the dead fire."

"If we didn't, they'll have awful headaches when they come around," said Tracker. "Here, look at this," and he showed them the weapon that he carried at his belt. A smooth piece of granite the size and shape of a large turkey egg was fastened to a wooden handle with rawhide wrappings.

"If you were cracked on the head with that, you could be very dead," said Broken Stick, "and if they're not dead, they'll have a hard time of it. We took almost everything they had." A spear, a bow and arrows, and two stone knives were laid before the boys. "And I opened their food pack."

Tracker handed each of the boys one of the knives. "These are yours to keep," he said. "You can show them to your friends and, maybe, brag a little."

"How did you find us?" asked Sheep.

"We picked up your tracks at the cave where you spent the night, and followed you all day yesterday."

"Must have been hard," said Sheep. "Those men knew you were behind us, I think. They made us walk in the hard places so as not to leave tracks."

"It was easy. We followed the bear. He was running loose and left good tracks. We were close behind when you made camp last night, but we waited until everyone was asleep so there'd be no trouble."

"I'm glad you found us," said Cricket.

"If we hadn't," said Broken Stick, "you'd be well on your way to being slaves to the plains people. How would you like to pack and carry for them, and sleep in skin tents when it snowed? How would you like to be up to your belly buttons in bloody bison hides at the fall hunt?"

"I guess now I'll never get to see a bison," said Cricket, and he laughed. "One thing, though—we found out that they didn't have Snow Flower. I wonder if we'll ever find her."

The middle of the following day at the village found Cricket facing the stern faces of his grandfather and mother. "We thought you were dead, son," said the old man. "We all know you shouldn't have gone, and it was a crazy thing you did. You should be punished, but I know, somehow, you felt you might find your sister. Just stay close now and keep out of trouble."

"All the children are down from the fields now," said his mother. "There are two older boys there watching. They will keep the deer and the antelope from eating what we've planted. You needn't go back. We're glad you're home.

"If you saw no sign of Snow Flower after following the plainsmen, then we don't know who took her," said Basket Woman. "It has been four days now. There's not much hope now—is there?"

Chapter
FIVE

S ummer was upon the earth, and in the canyon country the silence hung like a heavy broth. Each
morning, as the sky gathered light in the east, the
silence was shattered by the doves. These small,
pearly tan birds, no bigger than robins, lived and
nested and mated in the small wind caves high on
the canyon's walls. Doves cooing in the morning
sound like small, singing girls, practicing their "ooohs," yet when
the sound bounces around and echoes off the hard, slick face of
the cliffs, it tends to build in volume until it's more like wild

wolves howling. This, then, started each summer day, and when the doves were ready, they flew pair-by-pair up and out of the canyon to their feeding grounds in the high country, making light whistling sounds with their wings.

Each day the sun grew hotter. Small clouds and cloud shadows passed over the country, and what winds there were missed the canyon bottom.

On most days, Cricket took his bear, and his flute, and his friend Sheep to a small secret cave they'd found, two bends down and away from the village. Sheep was now the owner of a small skin drum, and the two boys disturbed no one but the lizards as they practiced playing. Their music had some effect upon the bear. He swayed back and forth while sitting upright, and he waved his arms as he moved.

Once, during a gathering at the place of old men, the boys were asked by the grandfather to join the drummers. At the big drum were two old men; the three others were doing a shuffling back and forth dance, carrying hard-eyed rattlesnakes, one in each hand. This dance was done to show that man was brother to all things living. The snakes, somehow, seemed not to mind, and to really act like brothers. They raised their heads and did not strike, but listened, with their tongues darting to the rattle of the shaking gourds and the beating on the drum skins. Cricket's flute joined with the drumming, and the clear notes made strange, wild music from the rhythm. The bear, like a small boy showing off, waved his arms and made whiny noises. The old men laughed when it was over and said that it was good.

On one hot day that seemed hotter than the others, the two

boys and the bear took turns sitting under the small stream that poured from the cliff's face at the spring. "This feels good," said Sheep. "I wish it was a pool. Wouldn't that be something?"

Cricket said, "Let's make one! Maybe if we got some help, we could have a good one."

They found that everyone wanted to help, even the grandfather. He said, "Let's build it here at the low place."

They made a dam where the old man said they should. They brought rocks and laid them like a wall. They brought clay in baskets and tamped it firmly behind the rocks, and they brought sand, and they dug and they patted and they stomped so it would hold back the water. A ditch was dug from the spring. "It will take three days to fill it," said the grandfather. . .and so it did.

Every boy and girl in the tribe hollered and splashed and got very wet. None of the children could swim, but they were all great splashers. The grandfather, the old men, all the mothers and fathers came, and they all laughed. The grandfather said, "Why didn't we think of this before?" Everyone in the tribe knew that the pool was a happy thing. Cricket wasn't happy though. He spent much of his time sitting on the side of the pool thinking of Snow Flower. Where was she? What was she doing? How could things have been different?

The heat still dragged on. One day at the morning meal, Basket Woman spoke to the old man and the boy. "Come with me," she said. They climbed the ladders on the cliff's face and stood in the fields. "See how the corn is wilting in the heat. It needs water. There'll be no crop unless it rains."

Taking a handful of earth, the grandfather said, "See how dry it is." It was dry, like sand, and the wind blew most of it from his hand. "Unless we do something soon, the corn will die. We'll have to have a rain dance."

That evening the people gathered at the place of the old men. A huge fire lit their faces and cast a flickering light on the hard, curving arch of the cliff. The five old men sat in a semicircle, shaking gourd rattles and beating softly on the large drum. Chanting in a high, clear voice, Cricket's grandfather moved the sound into a quicker and more solid rhythm. A hot wind stirred the fire, and the orange light on the cliff's face flickered and jumped to the beat of the drums. From where they were sitting in the shadows, Cricket and Sheep worked their way through the crowd and sat with the old men. Cricket's flute and Sheep's drum joined in, adding melody to the wild beat of the big drum and the rattling gourds.

Three young boys, older than Cricket and Sheep, now came into the firelight. They wore fans of feathers, tied in back to their belts, and leggings made of the hairy hides of big-horned sheep, with clicking bones fixed to the wrappings. They wore carved wooden masks that hung low across their faces, and from their arms hung rows of braided hair and feathers. These boys were the dancers—thunderbird dancers—and they caught the rhythm of the pounding music and moved like low-flying birds around the fire. As they moved, they spread their arms like wings and shook them to make the feathers and the dog-hair streamers dance in the firelight, and this looked like falling rain. As they leapt and swayed, they shook the rattles, holding one in each hand, which added to the sound of the shaking gourds, the music of the flute, and the pounding drums. Everything worn or used by the boys showed that they were birds—the masks, the feathers, the leggings—and the clicking bones and rattles were the sounds of rain, rain beating on the earth.

No one knew just when it happened. . .but there he was dancing! The bear was dancing! Following the leaping, weaving boys in costume, standing on his hind legs, waving his outstretched arms, he waddled and hopped behind them around the circle of the fire. The people, watching, laughed and clapped their hands, and the noisier they were, the higher the bear leapt, all the while waving his arms. The old men now joined the laughing, and soon everyone but the bear was hollering and whooping so loud that nothing else was heard, not even the beating of the drums.

The hot wind coming off the desert stopped next day, and by evening, dark clouds were rolling toward the canyon from the west. And the rain came, soft, gentle rain that lasted through the night.

At sunset on the second day after the rain, the family was seated around a small fire near the entrance to their home. A stranger, an old man, came and stood before them. "I've come a long way," he said. "My name is Two Bones, and I look for one who was once called Runner. Now I think he is called Song Maker."

"I am Song Maker, and I know you," said the grandfather. "You come from the south, from the village in the Canyon of the White Crow. Come. Sit with us. We have just finished eating, but there's plenty left, and you must be hungry. What brings you this far north?"

"I come seeking rain," said Two Bones. "We saw the clouds move two nights ago, and it looked from where we were like you had rain here in the canyon."

"Yes, we did, and I think perhaps we can make it rain anytime we need it. Here, Cricket. Show the man your bear." The bear was brought. "This boy has a friend, and together with this bear they made rain for us," said the grandfather. "The boys make the music and the bear dances." Two Bones laughed, and the old man continued, "Tomorrow we'll go with you to your village. Cricket, go tell your friend Sheep that we leave early in the morning, and that he should bring his drum."

"It's a strange bunch," said Two Bones, still laughing. "But we'll take anything we can get to make it rain, for our corn is wilting in the fields."

So it was that the early sun of the following morning found the two old men, the two boys, and the bear well on their way down the canyon. As the sun rose higher, the walkers kept to the shade. Hot sand and bare feet made for slow going, but the stretches of slickrock were smooth and easy, and at these places, they made good time. Cottonwood trees and low willows were seen, and they found cool sand and sometimes brackish water.

"I know you brought meat," Two Bones said. "We'll stop here and eat. There's a trail that goes up through the cliffs at the next bend, but there's water here, and shade." So they ate before climbing up the west face to the high country beyond. Once they were on level ground, they found it very dry. Even the flowers were wilted, and the hot wind stirred the low brush in sandy places. There was another canyon to cross, and it was near sunset when Two Bones said, "We're coming to our fields now. See how dry it is. We need rain, and soon." The walkers came to the Canyon of the White Crow and worked their way down into the village. It was a small, poor place of maybe five families, tucked in a crevice high off the canyon floor.

It was hard to see at first. The rock faces of the houses were light reddish tan in color—the same color as the cave and cliffs. They could see the dark window and door openings and smoke from cook fires. There were hides hung about, and stacks of wood—and they could see children watching. From the canyon floor, there was a ladder up to a narrow ledge, then more ladders and handholds up to the houses.

As they climbed the handholds and the ladders, the people saw them coming. The young children drew back and watched with big eyes when they saw the bear, but the older, bolder ones came closer. "Will he bite?" they asked.

"If you scratch behind his ears, he'll love you," said Cricket.

After a meal of cornbread and meat that tasted like that of the big-horned sheep, everyone gathered at an open place by a small fire.

"We make no promises," said the grandfather, "but several days ago we made rain in our village, and it was good. Now we come here to do the same for you, and we will try our best. So hope in your hearts when we call upon the gods of our people." He sat upon the ground and tapped his small drum softly. Two Bones came and sat beside him and began shaking a gourd rattle. Sheep and Cricket joined the old men, and the music of the drum and flute cut the night air. Sparks from the fire rose with a crackling sound and faded into the darkness. The grandfather's high voice began a chanting—a chanting to the gods.

Shouting and much laughter began as the bear appeared in the firelight. On hind legs, with arms outstretched and waving, he moved with a small, hopping motion. Round and round the fire to the beat of the music, as much as a bear can fly like a bird, the bear danced, and the people said "Oooh," and "Aaah," and the children gasped with laughter. For a while, the music and the chanting seemed to keep the light from the flames bouncing on the cliff's face, and the bear's dance kept time with the beating drums. But then the chanting stopped, and the drumbeats and the music stopped, and the bear dropped to his four feet and came to Cricket and sat beside him.

"We've done what we came to do," said the grandfather. "Let's all hope the rain gods heard us."

The next morning, Two Bones climbed the cliff face to the fields with the travelers. Turning their faces west, they saw the dark clouds, hanging low and moving toward them, lighted by the morning sun. By the time the old man, the two boys, and the bear were climbing out of the second canyon, they could tell it was raining behind them at the village and soaking the cornfields. "It's good," said the grandfather.

As they walked, the old man spoke. "I thought the bear could do it without the other dancers. Just look at it raining over there! The rain gods look kindly on our friend here, and he's earned a name. He'll not be plain Bear anymore. He'll be Raindancer."

While walking along the sandy bottom of their own canyon, somewhere below the village, the grandfather stopped and pointed. "Look here," he said. "Look at our tracks." They looked at the footprints they'd made two days before, on their way to Two Bones's village. "Notice the cougar tracks on top of ours? Why, that old boy followed us halfway down the canyon!"

Each day as the dawn came, the people heard the doves greet the morning with their cooing and their whistling wings. The corn grew tall in the fields, and the women came to the spring with their beautiful jugs to fill them and carry them balanced on their heads up the ladders to their homes in the village. The two hunters, Broken Stick and Tracker Man, went off together, carrying their spears and bows and arrows. The old woman, hunched and limping, climbed the canyon wall on the way to gather wood again. Perched on a rock at the edge of the village, the two boys looked at the sky reflected in their pool below. "It's good," said Cricket, trying to match the voice of his grandfather.

Later, in their private cave down the canyon, Cricket was speaking. "I wonder if I'll ever see Snow Flower again. If the plains people didn't take her, who did? Our hunters found the tracks of two plainsmen. We followed them, and our hunters killed them. There were no signs that they'd taken her. Our hunters keep looking, and there have been no signs—nothing."

"Maybe there were more plainsmen than the two that we followed," said Sheep. The bear followed their voices, looking first at one, then at the other as they spoke. "But if those Wolfmen far to the south have her. . ." And they were all silent. Even the bear was silent.

Then Cricket turned and spoke directly to the bear. "So, my friend, you've got yourself a name. You're Raindancer now, and

you can make it rain whenever you want. Sheep, do you really think old Raindancer here can make it rain? Should we try him?"

"Let's try. I've got my drums, and you've got your flute. I think I remember the chant words your grandfather sings to the gods. How about it?"

Cricket stepped out of the cave. "The sky is blue. All of it we can see from here is blue, with no clouds. . .so why not?" And they hunkered down, and the drum struck a slow beat, and the flute followed. Sheep began the chanting, and the bear stepped out to a flat place below. Holding out his arms like a bird soaring, he humped around in a circle. This went on until both the boys and the bear were tired and the music stopped and the bear stopped dancing. "Now we'll see what kind of a rainmaker you really are," said Cricket. "I'll have to tell Grandfather, though, and we might all be in great trouble."

Sometime during the night, the clouds came rolling, blotting out the stars, and the lightning came, and the thunder came, echoing up and down the canyon. With each flash, the cliffs shone bright as midday, and the sky-cracking noise split the night. Then the rain came slashing. Young children screamed, and their mothers clutched them tightly. "There'll be a flood!" hollered the grandfather. "Everybody come help me pull up the ladders so they won't be washed down the canyon!"

The people ran every which way, and it was then that Cricket and Sheep bumped together. The bear was safe in his special house. "Look at it!" hollered Cricket. "I didn't think it would be like this."

When a hard rain comes to the high desert country, the thin soil held tight by the sparse plant roots cannot absorb or hold the water, and it forms a small web of ditches. The ditches grow into gullies, and the gullies into deep washes. The water tears at the earth, always seeking a lower level, and the lowest places are the deep canyons. When a small ditch, a gully, or a deep wash hits the edge of the canyon, the water comes pouring—dropping and splashing down the cliffs in great cascades and waterfalls, and a muddy flood comes tearing down the canyon. Great rocks, tree limbs, sand, and mud are pushed before it. The whole canyon floor changes. What was once a sandbar now is slick-rock, and new piles of rocks and tree limbs are washed up against the cliffs. The great spread of roots of the few old cottonwoods still clutch the canyon floor, but their lower limbs are laced with broken branches, roots, and other remnants of the high rolling water.

So it was, and the people of the village watched by the light of the flashing lightning as it came rolling and boiling. "Good thing we got the ladders," someone said, "or they'd be gone."

When morning came, the people saw that everything below them had changed. They could still hear the splash of water at their spring, though, and that was all that really mattered. The canyon floor was changed by floods most every year.

"It's gone," hollered Cricket. "Our pool is gone!"

The grandfather said, "You can build another. There's something else, though. Did you two tricksters and that dancing bear of yours bring this on, or was it Kokopelli?"

"It wasn't Kokopelli, Grandfather. It was us. We wondered if

the bear really was a rainmaker."

"Don't do it again—you might stir up something you can't control."

"I knew we'd be in trouble," said Cricket.

Chapter
SIX

The weight of the years hung like a heavy stone upon the old man. As he had grown older, time had nibbled at his body, and he became more and more dependent on the stick he used for walking. Only the thick summer heat that clung to the sand and slick-rock of the desert seemed to soothe the aches that came with aging. Before he slept each night, he sang a small thanking song to the Sun Father for the comfort from the summer skies.

There were times when he thought of the coming winter and

the cold winds that whistled along the bottoms of the canyons. And he thought often of the robe, the wonderful bison robe he'd brought from the trading post by the river. Each time he touched it and felt the softness of it against his hands, he wondered about the bison itself. Traveling the deserts, the mountains, and the canyons of his people when he had been a runner, he had come upon all the animals in these places, and he knew them. He knew the elk, the antelope and deer, the cougar, the bear, and the sheep with the big horns, but he didn't know the bison. He'd never seen a bison. It was much in his thoughts lately. If he was ever to see one, it would have to be soon because of his legs. Would they carry him—even with his stick—another summer?

Twice since he'd owned the robe, he'd been awakened in the night by a dark shape that almost filled the space of the small room. Reaching out to it, he could feel nothing with his hands. It was a dream. He'd been dreaming of the bison. And then he'd watched the shape disappear through the small door opening. That was when he knew that this was the time of the bison.

So one day, he sat with Broken Stick and Tracker Man at the Place of the Old Men. "You have seen my black robe," he said, "the one I brought home from the traders. Lately it has been on my mind to find and really see a bison. I know there are bison in the plains, far across the Far Blue Mountains. I've been told there are as many there as there are rocks in the river—and that would be a wondrous thing to see. When I was a runner, I heard once that there were bison somewhere north and west of here."

"Do you know the Old Woman Mountain?" asked Broken Stick.

"I do."

"Other hunters have told us that bison use the spring at the north end of this mountain. We've never been there because it's too hard to cross the river."

"One thought I've had," said the old man, "is that if I went to the plains, I might find some trace of Snow Flower."

"And you might get yourself killed," said Tracker Man.

"I know I'm too old and must depend on my stick to get around, but if I were younger, I'd try for the plains country. Well, then, it will be the mountain."

"The river runs fast, with much white water," said Tracker Man, "and it makes a roaring sound as it cuts through the canyon. That's why we've never hunted or even seen a bison there, because of the river."

"I know of a crossing place," said the grandfather, "a place where the canyon is wide, and where the river runs slowly. Once I sat there and watched some big-horned sheep pick their way across without swimming."

"Maybe we should go with you," said Broken Stick.

"I'd only slow you down. But one day I'll show you the crossing. It's a day's walk west of here, along the rim of the canyon."

After talking with the hunters, the old man knew that he would go to the crossing, but first there were things here in the village that he had to attend to. And so he called the boys, and they came and sat with him. As always, the bear was with them. As the old man talked, the bear moved close beside him, content as the old hands scratched the hard-to-reach place behind the ears.

"I have it in my mind to see a bison," he said. "It's a thing that has been with me since I brought the robe home from the traders.

I must go soon so that I'll be back before the harvest. I know I shouldn't take you with me after you caused the big flood, but I'm used to traveling with you. Besides, you can help me cross the river. I think you're old enough and big enough for the trip. Will you come?"

"We'll come, won't we, Sheep? Can we bring the bear?"

"You may bring him."

The boys were excited now, and the questions came fast. "Where are we going? How long will we be gone? Will we see the place where the plains people live? Will we cross the Blue Mountains? Is there snow up there?"

"Slowly, slowly," said the grandfather. "We're going north and west of here, and we'll be crossing the river. First, though, there are things to do before we go. Have you noticed how dry it is? Tonight we'll hold a rain dance here in the village. You two spread the word and get some wood up here for a big fire. Go now and prepare yourselves."

The afternoon heat made a shimmering in the air above the rocks and sand of the canyon floor. There was no wind, and all living things had found shade. But as the boys worked with the wood, there were no thoughts of sun, or heat, or anything but the coming trip to see the bison.

"How big is a bison, do you suppose?" asked Cricket.

"My father told me they're bigger than elk. They're fatter, though, and have shorter legs," said Sheep. "He's never seen one, but he talked once with the people from the plains country at the trading place."

"We'll both be scared when we see one, and I bet we'll run and hide." The boys both laughed. "We'd better get on with hauling the wood," said Cricket.

Meanwhile, the old man was busy with things that needed doing at the village. He spent time that day at a home where a small girl had a soreness in her throat. When he entered, she was clutching a small corn-shuck doll, and her mother held her closely, singing to her in a low, soothing voice.

"Bird Woman," he said, "I have come to help. How long has she been this way?"

"Two days now."

"May I hold her? What name do you call her?"

"She is Smile Maker. . .but now she's not smiling."

"Take these leaves and stalks of blackbrush," he said. "Go now and make a brew of them, and I'll hold her till it's done." And he took the child, who searched his face with her large, dark eyes. "Here," he said, "hold my thumb and help me sing." He started chanting, and the child's eyes found his, and they sang there together until the mother came with the tea.

> Little girl with the dark eyes,
> I hold you on my knee,
> And we sing together
> While you hold my thumb.
> I look into your dark eyes
> And know you carry
> The future of our people
> In your small hands
> And in your smiling eyes.

So, smile at me
While you hold my thumb,
And while we sing together.

"Add some of this," he said, and he handed the woman wild honey that had turned to sugar. The small girl drank the tea, cradled in her mother's arms. "Tomorrow she'll be herself again," he said, and left them.

People remembered the fire that night because they could see a full moon from the Place of the Old Men. They saw the sparks fly up and mix with the moonlight, and they saw the shadows dancing on the rough face of the cliff around them. The bear danced well. The wild notes from Cricket's leg-bone flute joined the high-pitched chanting, filling the whole night with a wondrous beat. They watched the fire die, and they cried, "Oooh! Aaah!" Then the bear came and sat near the big drum, and there was a good feeling among all the people of the village.

The next day, the rain came, and all the things the old man had planned to do were done. Now he could go see the bison, if he could find them.

The morning they left, the village smelled clean and fresh from the rain the day before. Their packs were light, mainly blankets woven from feathers and rabbit hair. Each one carried a small jug of water, for there was much dry country between the village and the Mountain of the Old Woman. They all carried stone knives, and Cricket had his flute and the spear made and given to him by his father. The weighty part of their packs was dried meat from Basket Woman's storeroom, enough to last for the time they would be gone. Among the grandfather's things were rope, and a small bow, and sticks for making fire. While they walked, the bear roamed free, sometimes in front or following behind, always poking his nose into something and exploring as they went.

From the village, they traveled mostly north, following the canyon bottom. It was either deep sand or slickrock, and they wove their way among the boulders that lay scattered by the floods that came each summer.

At the head of the canyon, they climbed up through some small cliffs, and the whole sprawling, broken land spread out before them. They stopped and looked, and the boys stood wide-eyed in wonder.

"It's big," said Cricket. "Bigger than any place we've ever been."

"I've never seen so much sky before," said Sheep. "Not all at one time, anyway."

"If everything we see before us was the whole world," said the grandfather, "it would still be a big place. But what we see is only a small part of it—like one fist-sized rock in our canyon." They sat a while, just looking.

Mesas with flat tops, tall standing rocks like crooked fingers, rolling stretches of bunchgrass and sage, hillsides covered with piñon and juniper—all this lay before them. They could see gullies and deep canyons cutting the earth, slickrock, sand, and the green of the yucca with dead spikes standing. On the far horizons were cliffs showing light blue and purple as they blended with the sky. And the sky was clear blue this day. Nothing disturbed the high arch of it, except to the east, where they could see low clouds lying on the tops of the Far Blue Mountains, all that was left of yesterday's storm.

In all this space, there was no movement, except where a small wind stirred waves in the bunchgrass, and a lonely dust devil made a whirling in the sand.

"You see the cut in the land there where the low cliffs lie? That's the big river with the deep canyon, where we're going. We'll go now. It may be a thirsty walk, for there's no water between here and the crossing."

So they climbed the rolling hills and crossed the canyons and gullies. They walked through waist-high, soft-smelling sage, and bunchgrass that whipped their legs in passing. They plowed through sand and passed the night-blooming sand lilies, and they came upon sweet patches of crimson beeweed, and barberry, the green holly of the desert, and several kinds of prickly cactus.

The sun was still high when they came to the edge of the deep canyon. Far below, they could see the silver ribbon of the river. "I've never looked so far down on anything in my whole life," said the old man, and the boys answered by sucking in their breath as their eyes followed the maze of tall cliffs reaching up toward them.

"We'll sit here a while," said the grandfather, "and rest my old legs. Maybe even have some of Basket Woman's meat, and a sip of water from the jugs." So they sat, and when everything was still, they could hear the faint sounds of the river far below.

Most of the day they walked, staying close to the canyon rim.

Once they disturbed a red-tailed hawk that was sitting in the branches of a broken piñon. He cried a wild, high-pitched keening sound and sailed off over the great empty spaces above the canyon. "If we could fly like that, we could go straight to the Mountain of the Old Woman, see our bison, and be back here before dark," said the grandfather.

Sunset found them at the place of the crossing. "Gather wood, my friends. This is where we spend the night. We'll spread our blankets by the three tall rocks. They'll protect us from the wind."

The canyon widened here, and the river ran slow and easy, but it was much higher than years ago when the grandfather had watched the sheep cross. "That's Old Woman Mountain over there," he said, pointing with his hand. "You only see part of it from here. On the north end is where the hunters say there are bison. If we can cross the river, it's where we'll be going."

"It's a mighty big river," said Sheep. "Look at it! Do you think you could throw a rock across?"

"I think so. . .but not tonight," said Cricket. The bear was playing in the shallow part, running and splashing. He was having a wonderful time.

"Just get the wood," the old man said. "Maybe if I take a walk along the shore, I can find the things we need for our crossing tomorrow."

After the meal, they sat at the small fire until the stars came out and filled the sky with a wondrous glowing, almost like moonlight. A night bird called from across the water, and they found their blankets. Sleep was easy.

The sounds of the river woke the grandfather the next morning.

He lay there, listening to the water running over the rocks and lapping at the shore. Living in the dry desert country for so long, he'd almost forgotten these wonderful sounds.

The light was breaking in the east when he roused himself and woke the boys. "We have a big day," he said, "so let's begin," and he stirred up the small fire from the night before.

While eating some of the meat from the packs, he spoke. "When I was here many years ago, the water was low. I think I could have walked across. But now it's running deep from the snowmelt in the high country. There is another way, though. When you're through here, I'll show you how." They soon finished eating, and he led them up the river to a great tangle of driftwood. Here were broken trees, and branches torn from the banks and washed down through the canyon in flood time, piled high on a sandbar that he'd found the night before. "From these old trees, we'll build ourselves a raft," he said.

For most of the day, they lifted, pried, and carried. By late afternoon, there were three logs lying side by side in the shallow water, bound together by ropes from the old man's pack. When it was finished, he stood back, looked it over, and said, "It is good. We'll tie the packs on so they'll stay dry."

"This will be fun," said Sheep. "Maybe the raft will take us clear down the river."

"The first rough water would wipe us out," said Cricket.

When it was the grandfather's turn to speak, he said, "As we start, I'll want you both in back. Once we reach a place where it's too deep to walk and push, hold tight to the ropes, lie flat, and kick hard with your feet. We'll tie up the bear in front. He can swim and help pull us across. I'll ride when it's deep and push with this pole. All right? Now push!" And they were off.

When the grandfather had been a young man, he'd spent time at the main village near a river. He was a good swimmer and knew the ways of running water, so it was no surprise to him when the current caught them. Everything went as planned. The boys kicked, the bear paddled hard, and the old man straddled the logs and pushed with his pole. The raft was headed down the river, pulled sideways by the current, but was slowly moving toward the far shore.

"Hooo-ha!" hollered Sheep.

"How about fast?" cried Cricket. "Will it go any faster?"

There came a time when the raft slowed some, and they'd passed the slow drag of the current. "Can you touch bottom?" yelled the grandfather. They could, and the raft was pushed to shore. "How was the ride?" he asked.

"It was great!"

"While we're all in the water, let's push the raft up the river, across from where we started." This was done by heavy pushing, and by dodging rocks and potholes along the way. Then the raft was dragged high on a sandbar, and the old man untied his ropes. "Now we'll have a way to cross when we return," he said. "We're over the river, and it's late, and we're all tired. We'll rest here tonight."

"It was easier than I thought it would be," said Sheep.

Morning found them well on their way to the Old Woman Mountain. They traveled the rough country, making their way between huge boulders and dry gullies that lay in their path.

There were no trees here, nor plant life of any kind. It was mostly sand and slickrock. Everything was laid bare by storms that washed off the foothills now showing in the distance. It grew hot as the sun stood higher. "Don't drink from your jugs unless you have to," said the grandfather. "There may be no water until we reach the mountain."

It was almost dark when they got there, and they spent the third night at a dry camp at a place where the mountain rose high above them. Here there were no night birds calling. The silence settled like soft smoke.

Next day they made their way along the west side of the mountain on trails made by the wild things that sometimes traveled there. Sage and rabbitbrush grew on the hillsides with juniper, piñon, and oak brush. Higher up the aspen grew, now showing the dark green leaves of summer. The trail crossed a rocky gully cut deep by storms that rode the mountain. Here they surprised two deer that bounced up through the brush. They had been grazing on some low willows beside a clear-running spring. The water was cool and sweet, and felt good when they splashed it on their faces. The bear lay in it, drank some, and finally got to his feet and shook himself.

Late in the afternoon, they came to a rise, a place where floods had once torn great chunks of earth and boulders from above and strewn them on the desert floor. The old man had grown tired from the hard, rough walking and asked to sit and rest a while. From here they could see the end of the mountain and the end of their journey.

While they were sitting there, a great bellowing and clatter of rocks was heard. Over the rise he came—a huge bison bull, mean and mad, and dripping blood from an arrow half-buried in his side. The old man's first thought was that now he had seen one . . .he had seen a bison!

It was heading straight toward him. The old man thought about how mean the animal looked, and how big he looked—and the closer he came, the bigger and meaner he looked. The great head, with sharp curved horns and sparks for eyes, came closer and closer, and the old man stood in a daze, like a rock, like a stump with anchored roots. There was nothing but the bison. Just him and the charging bison. What happened next was very blurry in his mind. It was like a planned thing—like a wild and deadly dance with someone calling the steps.

The bull was almost upon them when the bear crossed, running almost under the old man's nose to his right. He turned to follow the bear. Cricket crouched and threw his spear, the point piercing the muscles between the bison's neck and shoulder but leaving the spear's shaft dragging. Then Sheep came running, crossing the bull's path. The bull slipped to his knees as his head turned. In falling, his great weight drove the spear's shaft into the ground and the point deep into his body, where it pierced his heart. And he lay dying on the ground—so close they could feel his spirit leave him.

Then they were surrounded by hunters—as many as the fingers on one hand. They had spears and arrows pointed toward them. One notched an arrow in his bow and aimed at the bear. When Cricket saw this, he charged—hit the bowman with his body just at the knees, and both hit the ground, the bow flying through the

air. The man was quick, quick as a striking snake. He was on his feet, holding Cricket by his arm with one hand—and holding a sharp stone knife in the other, ready to slash.

Things happened very fast, and now the old man stepped forward, his arm held high, palm and fingers toward them. "We come in peace!" he yelled. "Do you understand my words?"

"We understand you," said one who seemed to be their leader. "My name is Hawk Tail."

"I am Song Maker. I come with my friends from below the great river. I am an old man who wished before I die to see a bison."

Hawk Tail smiled. "Now you've seen one," he said. "If you come from so far, how is it that we understand your speech?"

"I am keeper of the wanderings and legends of our people," said the old man. "Many years have passed since cousins of my grandfather's grandfather crossed the river to find new homes in the north. You must be from those clans—maybe even distant relatives of mine. So, we ask that you let us come in peace."

"You travel with a bear?"

"He is the bear of my grandson. He's smart and can dance when we ask him."

"You say you are a song maker? Do you know the plants to use, and the songs for healing? We have one at our camp near the big spring who was crushed by the black bull lying here with your spear in him."

"The spear is my grandson's. He will never be a hunter because of the blood. He gets sick when he sees it."

"He's a better hunter than I am today. That's my arrow sticking in the bull's side. You didn't answer me about the healing."

"I am a healer," said the old man. "I know the plants and songs."

With their knives, the other hunters were skinning the bison while the boys and the bear stood nearby watching. One came over and handed Cricket his spear. "You are a big hunter," he said.

"That's the first thing I ever killed," said Cricket. "I just threw the spear without thinking. I was very scared."

"One day you'll be a hunter."

"My grandfather thinks I'll be a flute player."

"We will go now," said Hawk Tail, and the travelers left with him, leaving the hunters to their butchering. It was not far to the end of the mountain and the spring. The spring itself came from a rocky ledge part way up the hillside. It came down in a small, clear stream and sprawled out where the ground was flat. The bison had churned this part into a muddy wallow. Off to one side was the camp of Hawk Tail and his hunters. Here they had made a bower of sorts, with poles and branches to keep out the sun and part of the rain if any fell while they were there. Nearby was a rack made of poles tied together, where strips of meat were drying in the sun. Two men were at the camp—one stood and watched, and the other lay on a hide under the bower. There were two dead elk hanging from trees just out from the bower. The travelers made their way to the man lying on the hide.

"This is a song man, who has come with his friends from across the river to the south," said Hawk Tail. "He's come to help you."

The old man reached out to him. "Where are you hurt?"

"It's my leg, and here," he said. "I think some of my ribs are broken."

The old man felt the leg and ran his hands over the man's body, resting on the rib cage. "I'll be back. Maybe I can help you."

Among the trees by the stream, he found the sticks he needed and handed one to each of the boys. "Take your knives," he said, "and make them flat. Make them thick as my thumb." He gathered leaves from the low willows and made a brew of them in a pot he got from Hawk Tail. Then he returned to the man in the bower. "What do they call you?" he asked.

"Red Bull," the man said. "I found I'm much slower than the bull that caught our arrow this afternoon. I thought he'd kill me for sure."

"Well, Red Bull, there are two bones between your knee and ankle. One of these is broken. I can feel it when I touch your leg. The bone is sharp on the ends, and it is piercing the muscles when you move. Help me now. Hold tight to your knee with both your hands." And the old man pulled and twisted the ankle until he heard and felt the two broken ends come together. "Hold still, now, while I bind it." He laid the two flat sticks one on either side of the leg, and bound them with cord. "Tomorrow we'll finish the leg and bind the ribs. There is an elk hide soaking in the stream to make it soft." The brew was brought, and Red Bull drank it. "Lie back now." The old man laid his hand on the splinted leg and sang a song of healing.

Before sunset, the hunters returned with the meat and hide of the bison. A fire was built for cooking. "You'll like the liver baked against the coals," said Hawk Tail, and the travelers found it very good. "When we first talked today, you said the bear was a dancer."

"If he dances tonight, it will rain tomorrow."

"This I must see," said Hawk Tail.

"So it will be tonight."

Later, when the fire was built up, the grandfather called the boys. "Bring your flute and the bear, Cricket. Hawk Tail will see a rain dance."

"We brought no drums," said Sheep.

"Without the drums, there may be just a sprinkle," the old man laughed.

So they gathered at the fire—the hunters, the boys, the bear, and the grandfather. And the old man stood and held up his hand. "My friends," he said, "when we sing and play and the bear dances, sometimes we can make it rain. Hawk Tail said he'd like to see this happen, and we'll try. This is the first time we've done this without our drums, and we make you no promises. So, now we begin."

The wild music of the flute was heard, and the old man joined with a wailing chanting. Sheep began slapping at his leg, making a cracking sound in time with the words and music. And now the bear rose to his hind legs and waddled to a flat place near the fire. He raised his arms like the rain bird and moved in a circle. Cricket picked up the beat, and the bear danced wildly. The hunters laughed and cried, "Hooo-ha!" and they all began slapping their legs in time with the music. "This will do," thought the old man, and he joined in the slapping. This whole thing was all new to the hunters, and they laughed and had a great time.

When they ran out of music and firelight, the dancing stopped. Hawk Tail rose and came toward the visitors. "This has been good," he said. "You are fine people, and the boys are great hunters. You, old man, have done us a great thing with your healing.

"The men have prepared gifts for the boys. Each will have a horn from the bison. The hide will be taken to our village, where I will have our women prepare it for you, Song Man. I will bring it to you in your village before it snows this winter. I would like to see the stone houses where you live. They must be very grand. Our own poor village is spread up and down a good stream in a wide valley two days west of here. Our houses are waist high below the ground. We roof them with poles and brush, then sometimes cover them with earth. Our women raise corn and squash, and we have the dried meat from our hunting. I hope one day you'll come visiting. Bring the boys and the bear. The bear is a great dancer and has made us laugh tonight."

When morning came, the old man got the elk hide from the stream and cut it in long strips. With these strips, he bound the leg and chest of Red Bull. "When this dries, it will pull tight and become hard. It will hold your bones in place while they mend."

"Come see, Old Man. It's raining," said Hawk Tail as he came into the bower. And they sat that day and talked as the rain washed the earth.

"Tomorrow we must leave," said the grandfather. "I am very glad we saw the bison."

Sunrise was sharp and clear. The rain had left the earth smelling clean. "Come and bring the boys. There is something you must see," said Hawk Tail, and they climbed along the small stream and up the mountainside. Far in the distance on a plain of waving grass was a great herd of bison. They were grazing and slowly making their way toward the marshy wallow down below.

"I have seen them," said the old man. "I have seen the bison. I am happy."

Three days later, they were at home in their own canyon.

Chapter
SEVEN

The rebuilt pool was bigger than the one before, and the people, young and old, splashed and hollered and set the canyon ringing. The high heat of summer came upon them. Even the nights were hot, and what breeze there was rustled the leaves of the corn in the high fields but passed over the low-lying village.

There were more visitors. Another friend of the grandfather, Lame Eagle, of the village in Cougar Canyon, came. And there was old Lone Walker of the Hummingbird Clan, whose village was in the Canyon of Many Springs. "How do you hear of us?" asked the old man. "How do you know we can make it rain?"

Lame Eagle answered him. "Rain is very small this year, and the corn withers. Word gets around like hope, and I heard from a runner that you people with your dancing bear can suck water from a blue sky."

Lone Walker smiled when he said, "I heard it from a hummingbird. Somehow they seem to know."

This meant two more trips for the rainmakers. Their music split the heat of the fires in the two strange villages, and the children laughed at the bear when he waved his arms and circled, dancing like a bird. Something new had been added. Basket Woman, Cricket's mother, had made sleeves for the bear. Sleeves of soft, white leather, where she had fastened feathers and long streamers of white underbark from the cottonwood trees. When the bear danced, this hung low and shimmered in the firelight like rain.

They had brought rain to the villages of Lame Eagle and Lone Walker. Everyone wondered how this could happen with nothing but music and a small, black, dancing bear, but they had been there and seen it happen. . .and they were happy.

When Cricket first brought the bear to the house, Basket Woman had had grave doubts about him. How would he fit into the way they lived, being cramped so closely in the village? Everything had worked out, though, and she thought of him as just another child, a hairy one. In fact, she rather liked him, and bragged about him to her friends. "He really can make it rain," she sometimes said.

The grandfather thought she'd taken to the bear because of losing her daughter. "It can be hard on a woman—losing a child stays with her always."

Up the canyon, past the spring, there was a small, snug cave where the old man sometimes went to be alone. Among the things he kept there was a small drum that he stroked with his hands while he sorted out his thoughts, or while he worked on the songs he used in healing. No one bothered him there, and no one came without permission. He sat there sometimes and recited the names of his relatives, long gone, or the former leaders of his people, going back many generations. He must pass this on to Cricket—and soon. Cricket was sharp and creative. He learned fast and had the mind of a poet or an artist. Sheep, on the other hand, was slower, but very steady. One day he would be a great hunter, or even a runner.

It was here one day that he thought back to the time of the bison. He remembered how the great bull lay dying. No one had sung over the bull to release the spirit—and a spirit that large should not be left alone to wander. He must, somehow, even this late, put it to rest.

With a thick sliver of flint and a pounding stone, he pecked at a flat, smooth place on the wall of his cave. Slowly there appeared beneath his hands the figure of a bison, showing light on the dark surface of the wall. When it was finished, he took up his drum, and while stroking it with his hands, he sang the dying song:

Old bison bull,

You of the plain
By the Old Woman Mountain,
You are dead now.
Dead from our arrows
And spears.
We took from you only
The meat and the hide
To feed and warm us,
But we left your spirit
To join those of your brothers,
And to roam with them,
And to eat
The green grass with them.
So go now to your brothers,
Far from the plain
By the Old Woman Mountain
And go now—go in peace.

The old man felt the presence of the bison fill the cave. Felt the warm air from it, breathing on his back. And he turned, and there was nothing but the emptiness of the cave. He knew that the spirit of the bull had been there with him, and he knew that it had not been properly released. One day he would do it. He would use paint and do it in a proper place.

To Cricket the summer seemed very short, what with all the trips they made. It seemed as if they were always coming or going somewhere. Altogether, by harvest time, they had gone to all the small villages of their people, and everywhere the people had made a great fuss over the boys and the dancing bear. "Here they come!" the children would shout. "Here come the rainmakers!"

Now it was harvest time, and the rain was no longer needed. The grandfather was very busy. First were the ceremonies thanking the Corn Mother and the Squash Mother for their help and goodness. There was much drumming, chanting, and the making of beautiful sand paintings, and there was dancing far into the night around the fire. The boys watched, and the bear grew wild when he was held tightly and not allowed to weave and sway in the firelight. "You'd spoil it for Grandfather," said Cricket. "You'd make it rain, and he'd be angry." So they either held him or locked him away in his little house.

Then it was time to gather the corn and the squash that had ripened in the fields. The old men went first and offered ground cornmeal and squash seeds in the four directions and to all the gods involved in growing and harvesting. The women came— they picked and carried—and when they were finished, they had all that was worth saving safe in the village. Corn shucks were saved to be used for bedding. The yellow kernels were stripped from the cobs and placed in earthen jugs, which were sealed and stored in the village granaries. The cobs were saved for starting fires. Every squash was picked and carefully carried down the handholds and shaky ladders to the canyon floor below, then up more ladders to the village. It was a lucky woman who didn't drop any.

The corn and squash that grew in the fields weren't all the

harvest. The women knew where there were roots and berries, and these had been gathered and stored in season. Now the seeds were ripe, seeds from wild grasses that grew in places the women had marked in summer. They took forked sticks and beat on the grass, and they caught the seeds that fell in flat, shallow baskets. These seeds were to be mixed in a type of bread that was served and eaten at special times.

So went the harvest. . .and when it was over, and everything was stored away from pack rats and ever-present small brown mice, the village had a celebration. All night they sat at the big fire, and there was singing and dancing. It was at the harvest party that the women danced while the men sang and the big drum boomed. The people rejoiced, and the noise echoed up and down the canyon. And the bear tore loose, and waved his arms, and joined the circle of dancers. While the tired people slept the next day, there came a gentle rain that put out the hot coals under the ashes of the fire.

The harvest was over, but the big celebration was yet to come. Every year, when the crops were gathered and stored, all the people from the villages came together in one place for a grand harvest dance. The villages were mostly deserted—everyone came who could, leaving behind only those needed to tend the sick or feed the dogs and turkeys.

This year the dance was to be held at the Canyon of the Dog Leg, near the box canyon with the good water. The runners had said so. Old Spotted Wolf, from the big village by the river, shaman of all the people, had said so.

Basket Woman at first didn't know whether she would go. All those mothers with lovely daughters, everyone so happy. . .

"You must come," said the grandfather. "It will do you good to get away. There will be music and dancing. It will be a happy time. Please come."

"One day we'll find her," said Cricket. "I hope you'll come with us."

As the grandfather had said, everyone who could was going—everyone. There was much to do, thought Basket Woman. How do you decide what to wear? Will it be the green rock necklace, or the shells? What shall we take to eat? We must bathe. We must comb the hair.

And so they started. They moved in single file, following the grandfather, who knew all the trails in this rough country from when he had been the Runner. The sun, though it cast the shadows of early autumn, still shone hot, and the walking was slow because of the very old and the very young. Most people carried packs and jugs of water; some carried small children. Early in the day, before the rising of the desert wind, they crossed places where there was sand, and the sand showed tracks of those who had passed the night before. There were tracks of small brown mice, tracks of birds and beetles, the looping track of a small sidewinder snake, and a place where a scorpion had dragged its tail.

As hot and dry as it was, there was still much life to be found in the desert. They passed wild flowers on the trail—purple asters as big as a woman's thumb, and small, low-lying sunflowers. The yucca's green cluster of sharp leaves still cradled the tall spikes that stood dry and tall, carrying a scattering of empty seedpods, and there was cactus, looking dead and dry but still able to reach and grab with its stickers. Basket Woman had seen patches of desert oak no higher than a tall man's waist, bearing huge acorns. We'll stop and gather some on the way home, she thought. They're very good when chopped and mixed with meat.

Several times that day, they had seen small herds of antelope that raised their heads and stood looking as they passed. There were snakes that lay coiled in the shade of bushes and tall rocks, there were lizards, and once there was a desert tortoise that tucked its head beneath its shell when a small girl touched it.

They were tired when the old man led them to the spring and the small stream of clear water. This was the same spring where Cricket had found his bear earlier in the year. Several small cook fires were lit, and the people drank the good water and prepared their evening meal. Later, when the blankets were spread and the people slept, Basket Woman lay there, looking at the stars and listening to the sound of the small stream chuckling over the stones. All the mothers will be there, she thought. Mothers with their pretty daughters. Oh, Snow Flower. I miss you so.

Then, far out in the darkness to the north, several coyotes sang to one another. . .and so passed the night.

The next day at sundown, the people, still walking in single file, came to the Canyon of the Dog Leg and to the box canyon with the good water.

Chapter
EIGHT

og Leg Canyon was a place of high walls and warm colors with a sandy bottom. Here and there were cottonwood trees, gnarled and twisted, still carrying the green leaves of summer, and there were barberry bushes growing against the cliffs. A seep of water bordered by small, low-growing willows crawled through the sand and rocks. This water came from a spring that lay tucked in a small side canyon—a place where wild things came at night to make tracks in the mud and muzzle the cool water. Old Spotted Wolf had chosen this place. . .and the elders said that it was good.

Although the place was much used by the people, no one had lived here long enough to form a village. In the summertime, great floods came and shifted the sands around, making it foolish and impossible to grow corn in the bottoms, and on top both sides were rocky and of such poor soil that nothing grew except junipers, piñons, scattered cactus, and low-crawling sagebrush. It was a wonderful place to hunt, though, and hunters from all the tribes came each summer and stayed in caves close by the spring. Mostly they stalked the antelope in the high country, but sometimes they were lucky and found a deer drinking at the spring in the early morning. At times, there were many racks made of branches used for drying the meat. Some hunters spent much of each summer here hunting, gambling, and visiting with friends.

In the main canyon near the spring, there was a huge bowl of a place where the people often held their autumn dance. Paintings and writings from other years were done in colorful clays on an undercut wall, facing south. Nearby was the place of the great fire.

This year the people came, and the villages mixed one with the other, and they spread their woven turkey-feather and rabbit-hair blankets on the sand under the trees and under the great arch of the sky. There was laughter and confusion as old friends and relatives found and hugged each other and tried to tell all that had happened since last year's gathering while still hugging. Great piles of wood lay where they had been tossed from the cliffs above, and small fires here and there spread the wonderful smells of juniper smoke and supper cooking. This year it would be good—Old Spotted Wolf had said so.

After settling her family, Basket Woman took the water jug and headed for the spring. Taking a roundabout way, she passed through the many groups of people, stopping now and then to greet old friends, always looking, looking at the mothers and their daughters. Much later she returned with a sad face and no water in the jug. She had forgotten to fill it.

Earlier in the day, a great dead cottonwood tree had been dragged to the central fire pit, broken, and made ready for the huge fire that would give light and purpose to the evening, and when darkness came, the fire was started and the big drum sounded. Small groups of people left what they were doing and gathered round, and the light shone on their faces as they stood or sat hunkered in the sand. The grandfather, joining the old men at the drum, smiled and moved his hands in rhythm with the others. As more of the old cottonwood burned, the flames leapt higher, and the sparks popped and rose on the smoke, and the beat of the drum grew quicker. Looking past the people and the fire to the canyon wall, the painted figures, some with round eyes staring, seemed to come alive, and as the flames leapt, they appeared to move and gyrate upon the wall, swaying to the beat of the big drum.

Old Spotted Wolf, dressed in a robe made of bobcat skins, rose to his feet and spread his arms wide. The firelight lent color to his long white hair, and to the necklace of green stones that hung about his neck. Now the drums stopped, and there was a deep silence, broken only by the crackling of the fire.

Finally he spoke. "It is good that we gather here at the time of the harvest's ending. The runners have told me that all the villages have done well, and there is much food in the granaries. They have also told me that the piñon trees above this canyon are loaded with pine nuts this year, to be gathered if you wish. So, my friends, we shall make this a happy time the five nights we're here. Each night there will be music and dancing here at the fire, and we will give thanks to all the harvest gods that have favored us. I know that this year's dance will be better than all the rest." The old man sat down, and the fire crackled, and the big drum began beating softly.

Two old flute players joined the drummer, and the clear tones made music of the beat, and two boys came, one with a small drum, and one with a bone flute. No bear was with them, though, as they sat among the players. No one spoke as their music blended with the others.

There was dancing, as the old man had promised, and the young people swung and twisted about the fire. Wild and colorful costumes with bones and feathers were the rule; some carried rattles, and some had painted their faces and bodies. Above the sounds of the drums and the flutes could be heard the chanting of one old man. The people not dancing took up the cry. "Hooo-ya! Hooo-ya! Hooooh-ya!" This went on until there was nothing left of the fire but a few live coals that glowed red with the rising night wind.

The next four days and nights would be hard on Cricket. He was torn between wanting to have a good time and having to watch the bear. "If he dances," the grandfather had said long before they had left their home village, "it will rain, and if it rains, the whole dance will be spoiled for all the people. So you have two choices: either you stay home and watch him, or take him and keep him from dancing."

Here Cricket was now with a bear that went almost crazy at the very sound of music. During the first night, Basket Woman held him while Cricket played his flute with the old men. Who will hold him while my mother dances? he thought. He felt lucky making it through the first night without any trouble.

Having the bear at the dance wasn't all bad, though. Cricket found, after having been to all the villages in the summertime, that he had many friends. People, old and young, spoke to him as he passed, and the children, especially, followed him, asking questions. "Will he dance for us?" "Is his name really Raindancer?" "Will he bite?" Cricket found that from among them there were many who were willing to hold the bear at the dance just for a chance to pet him. "Just don't let him dance," was all Cricket asked.

On the first day, the two boys, their mothers, and the bear joined a group that climbed the broken trail up through one wall of the canyon to the high country above. Old Spotted Wolf had said there were pine nuts there for the taking. So people carried food and baskets and blankets, and some of the women, including Basket Woman, carried jugs of water for drinking balanced on their heads. It was a noisy bunch that finally came to the forest on top.

Mostly, when you think of forests, you think of tall trees standing close together, very lush and green—but a desert forest is different. Low trees, more like large spreading bushes, are the rule, maybe as high as one tall man with another on his shoulders. The trees are spread apart. Each tree sends out roots that feed on the poor soil and what moisture can be found within its reach, so each tree is like a small island and stands alone. Juniper and piñon live in this high desert country, with sage, black brush, cactus, and broken tree limbs filling the space between the trees. It is a place of many rocks, where squirrels and chipmunks scrounge for nuts and seeds and dig their holes.

Among the villages, there were clear-cut ideas about what was men's and what was women's work. Gathering pine nuts belonged strictly to the women and children. So the women took their baskets and their blankets and their children, and scattered toward the piñons. The men broke into small groups and found shady spots beneath the trees, where they watched the food parcels and jugs of water. There they passed the day, playing games with pebbles and bones, chipping the flint they'd brought for arrowheads and knives, and talking and telling lies about the things they'd done and seen.

While the men lazed in the shade, the women went about the hot, dry work of gathering the nuts from the piñons. Pine nuts are brown, have hard shells, and are about the same size and shape as small beans. They grow in pinecones strung along the boughs of the trees. Gathering the nuts was simple. One person beat at the cones with a stick while others held blankets and caught the nuts as they fell. Sometimes, though, the cones held the nuts very tightly in a grip of sticky pitch. Then the cones had to be picked, laid on the blanket, and beaten until the nuts broke loose from the cone. The crushed cones were separated and tossed to the ground, and the pitch built up on a person's hands until the fingers stuck solidly together, the arms were covered, and the clothes ruined.

At the end of the day, Basket Woman, with the help of Cricket (and the bear), had a sizable pack of nuts. "This is enough," she said. "They should last us all winter." They found where they'd left the water jug with some men of their village.

That evening, when the group returned to the canyon, they found a nice surprise. The hunters had brought in two antelope and a small deer, and they were turning on spits above the coals of a large cook fire. "There'll be a feast tonight before the dancing!" someone hollered.

One thing about an autumn dance—it was noisy. Happy people shouting back and forth to each other, babies crying, old men chanting, flute music playing, and drums beating—all this made the air ring in the canyon, and the echoes bounced off the hard rock walls. The second night was given to the women, and they danced until the light pushed back the stars. Dancing and eating the meat turning on the cook fires kept things moving in the firelight until the people gave up and found their blankets beneath the trees. So went the autumn dance, and everyone said that it was good.

On the third night at the fire, Old Spotted Wolf raised his arms, and the drums were silent. "Hear me," he said. "Each year, we choose a person or a thing that has been good for the people. Last year the greatest of all, the Sun Father, together with the gods of wind and rain and all the gods that have to do with weather, ran wild upon the earth. It was a strange year, with burning sun and heavy wind and rain, yet when it was over, our harvest was good and our people were happy. So our council asked Tall Smoke to do a huge painting on the wall. This was done; it is there for all to see and remember.

"This year, there has come among us another strange and wonderful thing. Most of you know Song Maker of the Bear Clan—the older people will remember him as the Runner. When we were young, he ran with me and with some of the others who now have white hair. Song Maker has a grandson, Cricket, a small boy and a great hunter. He is one of the few among us who has seen and killed a bison. He said he was very scared and had much help from his friends when it happened. I think that it was a brave thing to do and that he is a great hunter. I have been told, though, that he would rather play the flute than hunt, and he has already joined our players at the fire each evening. There is a third person, a boy named Sheep, who is a drummer. Then there is a small black bear that dances, known as Raindancer; he belongs to the grandson. Most of you know this group as the Rainmakers. They have come into your villages when it was dry, and they brought you rain. Without them this year, I'm afraid there would be no corn or squash for the coming winter. So the council has decided to leave a picture here upon the cliffs, a picture of the Rainmakers. We have asked Song Maker himself to do the painting, and we shall all see it before we leave the canyon. I ask now that this group come into the firelight so we can know you. Please don't dance or play for us now—we need this good weather for our dance."

The grandfather stood where he was at the drum, looked all around, smiled, and sat down. The two boys, followed by the bear, came out in front where all could see. Turning, they faced the crowd. Cricket slowly raised his right leg and balanced motionless upon the left, his arms outstretched. Sheep did the same and grasped Cricket's hand in his. Now the bear came on the line and did exactly the same thing, reaching his paw to grasp Sheep's hand. And so they stood, and the crowd laughed and clapped their hands. Then the three turned to the right and did a somersault, and the crowd was pleased. First Cricket, then Sheep, then the bear stood on their heads and held the position while the crowd roared with pleasure. When the three marched off into the shadows, the crowd was still laughing. Again the drums and the flutes began, and the dancers came and danced. Before it was over, Old Spotted Wolf stood before the grandfather. "Tomorrow night at sunset, will you bring your family and Sheep's to our fire to eat with us?"

"It will be good," said the old man.

Next day in the afternoon, Basket Woman and Gray Mouse, Sheep's mother, gathered up the two boys and the bear. "You will be clean," said Basket Woman, and they were marched toward the spring. There they were scrubbed with sand to remove the marks of the pine nut harvest, and their hair was combed. Even the bear was fussed over to see that he was presentable. "Now you will stay that way until suppertime."

When they stood before Old Spotted Wolf's fire, Basket

Woman was at her very best. Wearing the white cloth wrap the grandfather had brought her from the trading place, her necklace of white shells, and leggings of sheepskin with the white sheep's hair showing—all this shone light against her brown eyes and dark skin. She'd combed her hair, and she wore it in a bun in back, tied with soft deerskin with green stone beading.

Gray Mouse was dressed as a hunter's wife should be. Her wrap was of weasel skins, taken by Broken Stick in the winter, when the animals' hair was as white as snow. She carried in her hand a beautiful jug, almost round, glazed white with black markings, and she gave the jug to Humming Woman, the wife of Old Spotted Wolf.

Basket Woman also had a gift. She held in both hands a pretty basket that she had woven. It was a rich tan color with a design of crickets in dull red. It had a matching cover, and when it was removed, everyone sucked in breath with surprise. Blue bread! "This was made of the blue corn that we grew this summer. Grandfather brought seeds from the trading place early this spring. It is from the people who live far to the south." At the supper, everyone tasted the bread and found it good.

After the meal, Old Spotted Wolf looked at Cricket. "Stand up, son," he said, and the boy stood. "Your grandfather says that your name is Cricket and that you are a flute player. One of our gods is a flute player, and he started out as a grasshopper. He is a great trickster and causes our people much trouble. Do you stay out of trouble, son?"

"Not always," said the boy. "While we've been here, it's been very hard. I know I'd be in trouble if my bear got going with his dancing."

"I want to see him dance and make it rain. . . but not here. When our dance is over, will you come to the head village so I can see it happen?"

"We'll come," said the grandfather.

Basket Woman laughed and seemed happy at the fire of Old Spotted Wolf, but Cricket knew that deep inside she grieved for Snow Flower. Every night of the dance had been this way. And every night he had heard her crying as she lay on her blanket in the starlight.

In the afternoon of the last day, the grandfather gathered up the boys and the bear. "I want you to see this thing," he said. He took them to the cliff where he'd been working and showed them his painting. He had been busy. First he had gathered different colored clays from the canyon and mixed them with fat that he'd saved from the meat at the evening feasts. Then he had made paintbrushes from the pounded roots of the yucca plant, and now he was finished. "What do you think?" he asked.

"It's us!" said Cricket. "All four of us! Grandfather, you're the biggest, and we know it's you because you've painted an antelope at your head. You still think of yourself as the Runner, but there are birds at your shoulders showing that you really are Song Maker. Next is you, Sheep. See the curved-horn sheep by your arm? Everyone will know it's you. The next figure is me. See the thing by the shoulder? Isn't that a cricket, Grandfather? And the bear is tied to me, to show he's mine. It's a great picture; why didn't you make it bigger?"

"We stand very small beside the Sun Father," said the old

man. "He brings life to the world, and we can only stir up a rainstorm."

"How long do you think the painting will last?" asked Sheep.

"It will last a long time," said the old man. "More years than all of us have fingers and toes, including the bear."

"I will show you one more thing," said the grandfather, and he took them to a place across from the box canyon with the spring. There, in the cliff's face, and in a time long past, a huge rock had been torn away. Pieces of it could still be seen on the canyon floor. The shifting rock had left a hidden, room-sized space up and behind where it had fallen, and it was there the old man took the boys.

"You've been busy up here with your paint," said Cricket, for there on the smooth wall, they could see where he'd been working.

"It's a bison and two elk," said Sheep, "and there's a hunter."

"It's our bison, from Old Woman Mountain," said the grandfather, "and there's a reason I brought you to this place. Sit here in the shade if you will, and listen."

The old man sat back on his heels, his wrinkled hands folded over his walking stick. "Way back in time, in the very beginning of all things, Spider Woman was told by the Creator, our Sun Father, to make the animals and plants, and to make people. She did this with earth and spit, and she spread the mantle of life over all the creatures before her—and because we were all made from the same kind of mud, we were brothers and sisters. To all live things, she gave a spirit. It is said that the animals were made for the use of people, and that they were never to be

killed except for the food and comfort they provided for us who share their world. So, remember, when you take the life from any live thing, you take it from a brother or sister.

"When we killed the bison that day, we were excited and forgot that we had taken a life. This came to me one day in my cave, and I made a carving in the stone there, and sang the killing song. I was not surprised when the big bull's spirit came to me. . .and then left. I could tell it was not content, and that it still roamed free, not joining its brothers who had gone before. I promised that I would do a much better thing.

"This, then, is that thing. It shows the bison, along with the elk that were killed that day and hung at the camp. It also shows Hawk Tail with the bow and arrow. It was he, you remember, who started the killing. When I finished here, I sat and sang the song again. The spirit came, I know, and scattered dust and small stones about me. I have a good feeling, for now I'm sure the old bull is with his brothers, eating the tall grass in another world."

"You made the hunter look pretty small there beside the bison," said Sheep.

"Every time I think of the bison, I remember how big he seemed. He was huge—everything else seemed small," said the old man.

That night at the fire, the last night of the dance, everyone danced—everyone but the bear. He could only watch because he was tied tightly to a tree.

There was much hugging and saying good-bye the next day when the people packed and left the canyon. Basket Woman was going with her people to her own village. The grandfather and his rainmakers were going to the head village. Old Spotted Wolf wanted to see the dancing of the small black bear.

Chapter
NINE

They came in early evening to the main village near the river, where Old Spotted Wolf was the head man and shaman of all the people. For two days, they had walked with others returning to this village from the dance. It was a big place, spread up and down two canyons, both ending at the river. Old Spotted Wolf led the grandfather, the two boys, and the bear to a room where they were to spread their blankets. Everyone was tired, and after a small meal, they slept.

The cliffs facing east stood bright in the light of a new day when the village finally came to life next morning.

Humming Woman was preparing breakfast when the boys appeared with the bear. With her were Old Spotted Wolf and two others. "These are my grandsons," she said, and then, pointing, "This one is Owl Boy and that one is Striker. Maybe they'll show you around and keep you out of trouble until tonight."

Old Spotted Wolf spoke. "When darkness comes this evening, we'll have a big fire, and the people will come. Then we'll watch your bear dance and see if he can make it rain. I'll be keeping your grandfather busy most of the day at the kiva."

Cricket's grandfather now joined the group at the woman's cook fire, and he was smiling. "You're cooking fish," he said. "It's been many years since I've eaten fish. I had almost forgotten. And from the good smells, I'd say you know how to cook it."

"It's ready now, and for those kind words, I'll serve you first. Here you are. Now, boys, you watch those bones." The boys ate the fish and found it good.

"It's nice to be here again," said the grandfather. "Spotted Wolf and I grew up together in this village. This is where we ran together when we were young."

"Can we hold the bear and pet him?" asked Striker.

"He does not care much for petting," said Cricket, "but if you'll feed him some of your fish, he'll be your friend for life."

"There'll be food here all day if you get hungry," said the woman. They ate, and the new boys mauled the bear affectionately, and the old men talked of the times when they were young.

"What would you like to see and do while you're here?" asked

Owl Boy.

"I'd like to see the river," said Cricket.

Sheep said, "Me too, but first I'd like to look around the village."

"Let's go," said Striker. "Maybe today we'll swim."

Once, centuries ago, the cliffs here had been straight up and down, but water from floods over the years had undercut the stone, and great slabs of it had peeled off and been washed away to be ground to sand by the river. What was left in the face of the cliff was a huge arch that hung over a flat shelf, as high off the canyon floor as three men. On this shelf, the people had built their village. Now four boys and a black bear wound their way between buildings toward a ladder near one end.

Out near the edge of the great shelf, they passed a square hole in the flat surface of the floor; from it poked a wooden ladder. "What place is that?" asked Sheep.

"It's a kiva," said Owl Boy. "There's one here and one over there."

"What's a kiva?"

"It's a place for men. It's where they go to talk, a place where they have their ceremonies and keep their ceremonial things."

"Can we look down through the opening?"

"No. I've never, ever looked down there. It's only for the men. One day, though, when we're old enough, they'll ask us." So they passed on by and climbed down the ladder to the canyon floor. "This way," said Striker, and they walked down the canyon toward the river.

Every cave large enough and every undercut seemed to have

its buildings. In one cave, high on the cliff, so high that it took several ladders and many handholds to reach it, there were three houses that looked new. People were moving about, and a young boy waved to Owl Boy and Striker, calling out when he saw the bear. Others were eating or working at the cook fires. One young girl was nearing the top of the ladders, carrying a beautiful jug of water on her head. She didn't look down.

"How would you like to live up there?" asked Sheep.

"Not if I had to carry the water," said Cricket. The boys moved down the canyon.

Cricket and Sheep, during the spring and summer, had been many places and seen many things, but they were in no way prepared for the river. It was deep here, and far across, and it ran very fast.

"Do you really swim here?" asked Cricket. "It looks scary."

"Even our little girls come here. It's fine if you stay near shore out of the fast part," said Striker, and he dived in, followed by Owl Boy. No one was watching the bear. He went next and made small, happy sounds as he paddled away from shore. The three swimmers were splashing and hollering, "Come on in!"

"I've never ever been swimming, except in our little pool at home," said Sheep. "But we did cross a river once—remember?"

"I remember," said Cricket, and when the bear came close, he waded out and grabbed for the hairy back. The bear turned and paddled for the deep water, dragging Cricket, who was laughing and kicking his feet the way he had when they crossed the river with the grandfather. "Hooo-ya!" he hollered. "I'm swimming!" Then Sheep had a turn, and even Striker and Owl Boy laughed when the bear pulled them through the water.

Finally, after everyone was tired, they came dripping from the river, and the bear shook himself like a wet dog. Everyone lay resting in the sand. "Can he really make it rain?" asked Striker.

"He's done it many times, but we help some. If he danced now, the rain would come by evening."

"That might spoil it for Old Spotted Wolf," said Sheep. "He's got a crowd coming tonight."

"Maybe we can work it so he can watch the bear dance and see it rain both tonight. We'll need my flute and Sheep's drum, though. Owl Boy, can you bring them from our room without anyone seeing?"

"Grandmother told us to keep you out of trouble."

"You can tell them it was my fault," said Cricket, and Owl Boy left for the village.

"We'll be at our special place," hollered Striker. "Let's go this way." The two boys and the bear followed him down along the river. "Let's turn in here." He led them into a small side canyon shaded by several twisted cottonwood trees.

"This is almost as nice as our special place at home," said Cricket.

"I still don't think we should do it," said Sheep. "The old men will be mad."

"I have a very good reason," said Cricket. "Don't go spoil it." So they waited in the shade for Owl Boy, and when he came, they were ready.

They played the flute and the drum. Cricket sang a chant, the way the grandfather had taught him, and the bear held out his arms and danced in the sand. Bear tracks formed a circle, and wild music cut the air in the small canyon for as long as the boys could play and the bear could dance.

"Now you've seen it," said Cricket. "Don't tell anyone until after tonight. I've got a very good reason."

Everyone agreed it was a great night for the dancing. Old Spotted Wolf and the grandfather both said so when they came from the kiva. Humming Woman said so as she cooked the supper. No clouds could be seen from the village, and a soft wind was blowing off the river. People, both men and women, were adding wood to a huge pile at a clear place on the canyon floor— out from the ladders that led up to the village. "It will be dark soon," said Spotted Wolf.

The people came in great numbers, some sitting near the new-lit fire, and some where they could see from the village shelf near the two kivas. "We are ready," said the grandfather, and the drums sounded, followed by the clear tones of the flute. . .and from the shadows, all alone, came the bear. He raised up on his hind feet, held out his arms, and began to move. The people cried, "Oooh! Aaah!" clapping their hands to the beat of the music and the chanting of the old man. There was no other movement except for the leaping flames and the dancing, whirling bear.

Then from the direction of the river came a high wind and dark clouds rolling toward the canyon. The people heard the first sounds of distant thunder. A jagged gash of lightning ripped at the sky directly above, and the first drops of rain caused a popping in the dust. "That bear's good—and he's fast!"

hollered Old Spotted Wolf. The rain came hard, and there was great confusion, with people running for shelter.

The storm gods—those dealing with lightning, thunder, wind, and rain, having been stirred once in the afternoon and once in the evening on the same day by a small black bear dancing to music—turned loose all their forces. Never had the canyon country seen such a violent storm. The lightning ripped giant holes in the night with blinding light. Thunder roared and rumbled through the deep walls of the canyons, sound bouncing like that of a thousand drums, and the wind and the rain slashed at the people, who held their heads, some screaming into the night. This was the storm of all storms. No one had ever imagined such thunder and lightning as that coming on that night. For many years, it was known as the Storm of the Bear.

As the dancing and the music became scrambled with the running and the screaming, and the fire hissed and sputtered in the rain, Cricket grabbed Sheep by the arm. "Follow me!" he cried. "Keep your eyes on the girl there—the one with the white wrapping." They came behind the girl, one on either side, and the people moved and churned around them. "This way! This way!" cried Cricket. The three—two boys and one girl, all wet and dripping—came to a protected place beside the cliff.

"It's Snow Flower!" hollered Sheep above the sound of the storm.

"Oh, Cricket!" was all the girl could say.

When the bear found them, they had climbed the ladders to the protection of the arched cliff above the village.

"I saw you on a ladder with a jug of water this morning," said

Cricket. "I knew it was you, and I planned the raining. Will you run with us now? I think I can find the way to our own village, even starting in this storm and at night."

"No need to run. I'm free to go at any time—and I've been looking for you. News of your rainmaking bear has traveled fast, so I knew you were coming. Is Mother here, and Grandfather?"

"Grandfather is, but Mother went home from Dog Leg Canyon."

"I'm happy you've come, and that I'll see everyone very soon."

"How is it that you're here in the main village?" asked Cricket.

"I was rescued by a hunter named Blue Crane. It's a long story."

"We can sit here while you tell us."

Snow Flower put one hand along the bear's head, rubbing at his ears and talking as the rain fell on the hard rock surface just beyond their feet.

"I remember it was night," she began, "and in the starlight, I saw two men coming toward me. I thought it was our hunters, and they stopped. One picked me up and put his hand over my mouth to keep me from crying out. I was carried across the field, and they tied something over my eyes. It seemed a long time till they put me down. We walked over mostly slickrock, I guess, so we'd leave no tracks. They did not hurt me but were very cross when I walked too slowly to suit them.

"When they took the blindfold away, it was early in the morning. We were at a cave near a small spring. Two other men were there—one, I could tell, was a hunter, the other an old man. The old man was lying on some skins, and when he moved, he groaned as if he was in great pain. The first two men left—I think they went back the way we had come. Anyway, I was at the cave with the hunter and the old man."

"The first two—the ones who took you from the field—did one wear two feathers and the other one feather?" asked Cricket.

"Yes, that's right."

"We followed their tracks," said Sheep, "and they kidnapped us."

"But Broken Stick and Tracker Man killed them," added Cricket.

"They were rough-looking men," said the girl. "Anyway, I was at the cave. They fed me and gave me some skins to sleep on. They told me by signs that I had to stay with the old man. I would be followed and killed if I didn't. I know they meant it—the hunter pointed many times at the knife he wore at his belt. So when he left—to hunt, I guess—I left the cave to look around. I couldn't see anything familiar at all. I looked for the Far Blue Mountains but couldn't see them.

"So I went back to the cave, thinking maybe I could help the old man. He seemed in much pain and kept clutching his side. He could move around some but never went very far from the cave. The hunter came back late in the day, with some rabbits he'd killed, and he made signs that I was to clean and cook them.

"So—this is the way it was. I would watch the old man and do what I could for him while the hunter was away hunting. I tried twice to escape, but it was strange country, and I knew I'd get lost. Both times I returned to the cave.

"Being at the cave with these two, I knew that as soon as the old man was able to travel, we'd be gone. While I was with them, I learned some of their words, enough to understand what they were saying. They told me that I was nothing but a slave and that I would go to their country and help their women with things at their camp.

"I had been in the cave all summer and had gotten used to the old man. He was mean and cranky at times, for he was in much pain. One day I didn't please him in my helping, and he struck me. He hit me in the face with the back of his hand. I screamed at him—yelled at him in our language.

"That was when Blue Crane came. He came into the cave and took me with him. He said he'd been watching for several days. He thought I belonged somehow to the hunter and the old man, but something made him suspicious. When he heard me holler in the words of our people, he came, and I told him how it was—that I was being held there.

"Blue Crane was going to kill the old man, but I stopped him. I'm sure the hunter would be very angry when he returned and would come looking for us.

"Blue Crane brought me here. He lives here and takes care of his mother in the house with the long ladder, where you saw me. He is a good man and was going to take me home as soon as the people returned from the Harvest Dance, when he'd have someone to help care for his mother. Now I can go home with you. I can hardly wait. It's been a long time, and I've missed the village and my friends—and especially my mother."

Fall comes late to the canyon country. First signs are the cool nights, and the leaves of the cottonwoods turning a wondrous gold. You know, somehow, that this will never last, for soon the nights will be cold, and the leaves will be scattered by the wind.

The sun travels lower, more and more toward the south, casting longer shadows than it did in summer. The grandfather was almost looking forward to the wintertime—to when the snow came blowing across the face of the cliffs, to when he could use the thick bison robe he'd brought home from the trading place. He wondered sometimes if Hawk Tail would come before the first snow, as he had promised. It would be good to talk to him of the troubled spirit of the big bull killed on Old Woman Mountain. Also, there were many questions in the old man's mind about the hunter's people in the north.

Basket Woman was happy now after seeing Snow Flower. She knew her daughter wasn't lying dead somewhere, or with the cruel people far to the south. And the boys—no splashing in the pool now, nothing to do in the fields. They had heard once that if they followed the canyon to the very end, they would come to the river. Maybe they would do it, or maybe they'd build a fire at the opening of their secret cave and practice the flute and drum, maybe even learn some new chanting. And what about the rainmaking bear? For days now, he'd been curled sleeping in his bear house. He wouldn't be much use to anyone until spring.

The whole village had gone for several days to help the old Wood Woman gather great piles of dead piñon and juniper for winter, for the days when nothing could move in the deep snow drifting through the land, and everyone hollered, "Hooo-ha! I now throw the wood!" as it crashed to the rocks below. The old men looked once more to the granaries where the corn and squash were stored, and they said that it was good.

F
B

AUTHOR
BIRD, E.J.
TITLE
THE RAINMAKERS

DATE DUE	BORROWER'S

F
B

BIRD, E.S.

THE RAIN MAKERS